The Spirited Mistress
and Other Stories

A Collection of
Esar-Haden Tales

H. Rad Bethlen

Rooster & Raven

Library of Congress Control Number: 2024948847

For the Daughters of Zeus and Mnemosyne

Author Statement Concerning Artificial Intelligence

The way I write consist of several phases.

1. Idea generation.
2. Research.
3. Story development.
4. Outlining.
5. Writing the rough draft.
6. Editing and rewriting.
7. Editing and polishing.
8. Copy editing.

I will *occasionally* use AI during the research phase if I can't locate some bit of information on my own—but I try to locate it on my own first.

I will *occasionally* use AI during the story's development if I get stuck on something—but I try to resolve my own story issues first.

I *intentionally* use AI during the copy editing phase as a stand-in for a copy editor, which I can't afford to pay for yet which I don't want to go without.

A copy editor is the last set of eyes to look at a manuscript to check for grammar, usage, spelling, and punctuation mistakes. I ask the AI copy editor to make suggestions on corrections. I evaluate those suggestions. If I agree, I make the changes.

I don't use AI for anything else.

Be comforted that these stories were written by a human being for other human beings.

H. Rad Bethlen

The Spirited Mistress

The Way of the Samurai is one of immediacy, it is best to dash in headlong.

> - *Hagakure,*
>   Yamamoto Tsunetomo

Matron Mother Ufa stood on the top step, scanning the street below. This was her first public outing since consolidating her hard-won power. She had surpassed her sisters upon the unexpected poisoning of their mother. (By whom, none would or could say.) Maria stood alone nearby, isolated from the bustle. Ufa studied the body language of her youngest sister. Maria stood without confidence. 'If she looks weak, our house looks weak,' thought Ufa. She descended the steps.

Her sister turned, noticed her, and half bowed. "How was the reading, Matron Mother?"

"An excellent reading. Repina is a fine poetess." The matron mother reached out and gripped the chin of her youngest sister, lifting her head. "Where is our sister and the males?" Maria blanched. Her eyes showed fear and embarrassment.

"In the public house, Matron Mother," she stammered.

"Fetch her—now," hissed Ufa. Maria turned to leave but Ufa grabbed her shoulder, pulling the younger female close to her. "Comport yourself like the proud and powerful dark elf woman you are. Eyes are always on us." She released her sister.

Several other matron mothers emerged from the hall, glancing at her as they passed. Quizzical looks crossed their faces as they saw Matron Mother Ufa standing without attendants. Ufa maintained a cool composure as the line of matron mothers, their daughters, and attendants passed. None spoke to her. She gripped the handle of her sword to give vent to her frustration.

Maria reappeared by her side. A few moments later Halli and a coterie of males approached, accompanied by the sounds of laughter.

"Sister," said Halli. She hung on the arm of her favorite male. She had not yet learned the habit of referring to her sister as "matron mother," as she should.

"You're drunk," said Ufa.

"That's why I drink!" said Halli, laughing, as did her lover.

Ufa looked past the pair to the other males. They stood in stony silence. She looked around. She could feel the other matron mothers watching, judging, evaluating.

"Did they not serve wine at your little," asked Halli, motioning to the recital hall, "well, whatever it was you were doing in there?" She giggled, tried to walk and stumbled, pulling on her lover to keep her balance. "Let's get home." She began the short walk from the recital hall to Matron Mother Ufa's estate. Maria and the other males all looked to their matron mother. She nodded and they fell in behind Halli.

As Halli and the others approached an intersection they were blocked by a group of males who were loading a wagon under the direction of a female. "Out of the way!" Halli yelled. "Scum! I'm high-born. You're nothing!" She released her lover and began to shove the males. They struggled to keep ahold of their boxes and baskets. Rare foodstuffs from the surface spilled onto the street. Halli persisted, slapping and kicking the unknown males. Finally, the female, who belonged to a lesser house, but who was in charge of the accosted males, intervened with as much tact and self-control as she could manage.

7

"If you'll wait," she said, "it will be but a moment. As it is, you're delaying us."

Halli turned to her. "How dare you speak to me! Do you know who I am?"

The other female frowned. She looked at Halli, Maria, and the males. Matron Mother Ufa stood at the back of the group and could not be seen.

"I meant no disrespect. But if you will allow us to —"

Halli reached out to strike the woman, but in her drunken state she stumbled and crashed into the wagon. Her skin reddened. She reached for the dagger at her belt, steadied herself, withdrew the dagger from its sheath and squared herself against the merchant, wavering side-to-side. The two groups of males eyed both women, then exchanged glances. The boxes and baskets were set aside. Hands went to swords and daggers.

Halli lunged forward. The other female stepped aside, reached out, and slapped Halli in the face. "You stupid, drunken, high-born bitch!" she cursed. Halli backpedalled. She reached up and touched her lips. She pulled her fingers away and looked at them.

"You—you struck me," she said, astonished. "I'm going to—" She looked from her bloodied fingers to the female merchant. "You're dead!" She looked to the merchant's males. "You're all dead!" The males exchanged worried looks. Their eyes went from Halli to a new arrival.

Matron Mother Ufa had made her way to the front, sword in hand. Halli noticed that the attention of the males had left her. She looked and saw her sister, now her matron mother, although she did not properly recognize her sister's new authority, as Maria did. She held out her fingers and jutted out her split lip.

"Look what she did. She disrespected our house." Her eyes lit up. "Let's kill them, sister."

Ufa stepped forward. Halli looked away from her matron mother to the unknown female. "You ignorant fool," she hissed. "You'll regret—" A flash of movement caught her attention.

She shifted her gaze just in time to see Ufa bring her sword across in a tight arc. The blade struck Halli in the throat, slicing through meat and bone. A geyser of blood shot straight into the air out of her neck as her head rolled forward and off. Halli's body spasmed. Her limbs went ramrod straight, her dagger was flung from her hand by the involuntary action. Her lifeless body collapsed next to her decapitated head.

The two groups of males backed away, cringing in fear. The female merchant looked at the matron mother.

"A drunken fool," said Ufa. "An embarrassment—arrogant and weak." Ufa looked from her sister's corpse to the merchant woman. "She deserved to be slapped like the child she is," she looked down into her sister's face, "was."

"I—I meant no disrespect to your house."

Matron Mother Ufa spun. She thrust her sword through the woman, silencing her. She yanked the blade free. The woman fell, collapsing onto Halli's corpse. "But you did," she said to the dying female. She watched the life drain from the woman's eyes. None of the males spoke. Maria was silent.

"What house?" Ufa asked, looking at one of the unknown males.

"House Adal-Bör," he said, hastily adding, "Matron Mother."

"Give Matron Mother Elisa a true accounting of what happened here," said Ufa. She turned to Halli's lover, the male who had drunk with her. She pointed her sword at him. "Take this worthless male with you. Give him to your Matron Mother. I will make further amends. She may do what she wishes with him." She motioned with her sword. The male, his drunken haze swiftly clearing, parted from his companions and joined the opposing group. The males of House Adal-Bör put their hands on him, restraining him.

"Come," commanded Matron Mother Ufa. "This is the way." She turned her sister and her males around. As she passed the recital hall one of the matron mothers who was still present caught her attention.

"Matron Mother Ufa," she said and nodded.

Ufa smiled.

Trog

Esar-Haden stood—eyes closed—the weight and discomfort of his fetters forgotten. His eyesight was faulty due to malnutrition. If he were to open his eyes he would see gray blotches instead of a feast-in-progress.

The sounds of a feast: raucous laughter, the hissing of indulgent gossip, the grotesque grinding of mastication, echoed off of the walls, filling him with the contradictory emotions of longing and disgust. In a corner some fool attempted to defeat the cacophony with music.

He felt a woman's nails. They cut paths in the grime coating his chest. He opened his eyes. Like him, she was a dark elf. She was intimately close. Despite the availability of food, she was as skeletal as he had become. Her black satin top hung from her narrow shoulders like an empty rag. She wore a black leather skirt, heels that caused her to wobble, and a ridiculous amount of gold bangles. Her white hair hung limp, her ebony skin was ashen, her lips were parched, her eyes were red-rimmed. She threw an arm over him, her bangles singing, and sniffed him like an animal.

"You smell," she wavered, intoxicated, "of Baphomet. Are you he?"

"Yeah, I'm that long lost mother fu—"

"I knew it!" cried the woman. She flung herself backwards, her hips striking the overladen tabletop behind her, rattling the silverware, knocking over wine glasses, spilling their contents. "I beg you, lion of the labyrinth, most mighty of the minotaurs, reveal the secrets of your infinite maze! I shall make a thousand human sacrifices in your name!" She barely made it through her theatrics before she burst out laughing and spun to face her audience, who laughed along with her.

"Don't dare tempt him, Nin, he hasn't been brought here to be teased."

Esar-Haden recognized the voice but couldn't place it. He studied what patches of the room he could make out. The one called Nin spun and once more sniffed him. "But he smells worse than a rotting corpse. They couldn't bathe him before they released him?"

"I suppose once we bought his freedom, he and his stench became our problem, not theirs," jested the voice that was so familiar to Esar-Haden, yet the identity of its owner eluded him.

When Esar-Haden's eyesight had returned he sought the speaker and found him—hidden behind a suckling pig. "I must be hallucinating."

"Why, Esar?" asked the corpulent dark elf seated in a throne-like chair at the center of the long table. A human male stood just behind him, holding a green-tinted bottle, ready to refill his master's goblet of wine. He was from the surface, his pale skin reflecting the floating, magical orbs of light. A collar pinched his neck.

"I can't imagine why an enemy of mine would buy my freedom," said Esar-Haden. "Especially when I was soon to be executed."

"An enemy? I'm hurt. We've never been enemies. If I'm not mistaken, we were quite close at the academy. I recall the usual pranks, bouts of drunkenness, even—"

"Until you tried to have me killed."

"I never!"

"You've forgotten?" asked Esar-Haden. "I haven't."

"Why would I ever wish you killed?"

"I called you a half-breed."

The dark elf, Sirot was his name, was obese. He must have had some human blood in his lineage. There seemed no other way he could achieve such girth. Because of this he was mocked and ridiculed in the military academy, despite being from an important house.

"Oh, Esar, I've long forgiven you. I thought you'd forgiven me."

"No. I just haven't gotten around to you yet."

"Let me make it up to you." Sirot smiled. "Nin? Our unfortunate guest lags behind. Do hurry him along."

"You don't mean—"

"Oh, I certainly do."

Nin, who was still before Esar-Haden, turned and picked up something from a gilded platter. She turned back, a white cube pinched between her talon-like fingers, and lifted it to Esar-Haden's lips. "Let it dissolve on your tongue."

Esar-Haden leaned back. "Is that your game, Sirot? You want to poison me? Watch me die? Couldn't wait for my execution?"

"Oh, Esar. As if I would degrade myself. No, my dear boy, I mean to restore you. And then," he laughed, "we shall speak of why."

"I won't," said Esar-Haden, turning his head from what was proffered.

"I'll take one with you," said Nin, her grin making taunt the flesh of her angular face. She popped the white cube into her own mouth and reached behind her without looking. Sirot placed another cube in her palm. She offered it to Esar-Haden. "Take it, hurry. We can go together."

"You're insatiable, Nin," said Sirot, laughing.

Esar-Haden watched Sirot's jowls shudder as he laughed. He looked to the woman before him, studied her skeletal face, and decided he didn't care if he lived or died. He opened his mouth. She placed the cube on his tongue. It began to dissolve. He spoke as the cube turned to paste. "I'll be the first to greet you in Hell," he said to Sirot.

"Better think of pleasanter environs, Esar, and fast. I do hope you—" But what Sirot hoped for, Esar-Haden never knew.

A split second after he swallowed the paste he left his body and found himself on a desolate, rocky plain. The sky was red, as if a forest fire burned but there were no trees, no life at all in the desert of volcanic ash. A shadow moved but he lost it. A shape, perhaps a man in a ragged fur cloak, rose up and rushed toward him. He instinctively backed away but whatever it was it moved with inhuman celerity.

He yelled as the figure came to a jarring halt before him and in one movement threw back the cowl of the cloak with one fleshless, boney hand and with the other reached out, a gnarled-wood and rust-pitted steel scythe materialized from the sulfurous air. Esar-Haden had no doubt that he looked into the face of Death itself. He shut his eyes tight.

He heard a roar, but it did not sound like Death's predatory bellow, but the roar of a crowd. When he opened his eyes he was in a torture chamber as vast as a colosseum, with an audience of thousands awaiting the horrific show. The colosseum appeared to be made from the rib cage of an impossibly massive beast. The arc of the ribs overhead cast wavering-edged, elongated shadows. The bloodthirsty crowd chanted his name. He spun, looking for a way out. He was surprised to be facing a stone wall. The roar was gone.

He looked around. He was in a room. The flickering light of fire illuminated the space but it came with no sound or smell. The walls, floor, and ceiling were all sandstone. Painted hieroglyphs adorned the walls but he could make no sense of their jumbled, frenetic images. Men wearing tight-fitting white wraps around their loins passed by. They turned to look at him. Copious amounts of blood seeped from their pupil-less eyes, ran down their chest, and stained the fronts of the wraps. They opened their mouths but instead of sounds, a torrent of beetles issued forth, washing over him. He screamed.

There were other spaces, some indoors, some outside, some underground, some in landscapes so alien he could not comprehend them. But these marvels, these horrors became a blur, a rapid-succession of terrifying, fascinating, otherworldly visions that was beyond his ability to understand. Somehow the kaleidoscopic nightmare ended—followed by a dreamless sleep.

. . .

"They say begin as close to the problem as possible."

It was Sirot's voice. Esar-Haden opened his eyes. He was in a small, richly appointed room. His fetters had been removed. He had been washed. His nails had been filed. His hair, which had grown to his waist during his desolate incarceration, had been cut and treated, returning its natural luster. He must have been anointed with healing magic, for he felt better than he had since before his capture, torture, and imprisonment.

Sirot was seated on the bed next to him, studying his own manicured fingernails. The room was empty except for the two men. Sirot glanced at Esar-Haden. "I would have followed that implacable rule, except you had to know."

Esar-Haden scooted to a seated position, tucked a feather-stuffed pillow behind him, lifted his arms, and placed them behind his head. "Know what?"

"What it's like. We have several names for it. Most people call it 'trog,' or 'troggy.' Nin shared some with you. Tell me, where did you go?"

Esar-Haden looked up at the ceiling. Unlike most of the buildings in Pwyll, one of many cave cities inhabited by the dark elf race, this building was not made of cut stone, but wood. This informed Esar-Haden that he was in the Ghetto of White Skin. It was the only place in Pwyll that used wood (stolen from surface during raids) for construction. He had grown up in the Skin's alleyways and prostitute-choked streets. He knew it well. He pursed his lips.

"Ever shifting, ever fantastic." He glanced at Sirot. "Filled with horrors and dangers."

"Most likely the Abyss. Many go there." Sirot looked again to his nails, turning his hand over.

"Why would they do that?"

Sirot glanced at Esar-Haden. "I told you to think of something pleasant." He patted Esar's thigh. "The drug, trog, takes you places. A jaunt outside of your body. Astral projection. The destination depends on the traveler. Some few claim to have stood atop a mountain crowned with a temple made of pure white light. There they spoke with the wisest of the gods, drank mana from their cups, and learned the ultimate truths—unfortunately, forgotten upon returning. I myself have not been."

"A shame." Esar smiled. "If anyone deserves the mana of the gods—"

"Hush, Esar," interrupted Sirot. "Us dark elves are of a more despotic, bloodthirsty, cruel bent. I don't have to tell *you* this. So we often visit the Nine Hells, the Abyss, or even the Outer Reaches, where reason itself comes under attack. Not that these destinations are without their charms."

"I promised to be the first to greet you in Hell. Perhaps that's a promise I can't keep?"

"Me? Oh, no. I don't use."

"So you deal."

"Precisely," said Sirot. "You do catch on quickly, don't you?"

"I try."

"Well, and now we come to the problem at last." Sirot rose and began to pace the small room. "I've a good business here. Trog is becoming increasingly popular and yet," he spun and looked at Esar-Haden, frowning as he spoke. "There grows a dislike for trog. It affects females much more dramatically than males."

Esar-Haden smiled.

"Ah, you see where this is going?" asked Sirot.

"It threatens to upset the balance of power. If females are jumping the planes the males could revolt and strike down their tormentors, as they've conveniently left their defenseless bodies behind."

Sirot smiled. "We're not there yet and perhaps never shall be. Certain safeguards have arisen. You've touched the heart of the matter, though. Trog is despised by the ruling matrons. They sense instability, they find their daughters in altered states, unable to be brought to their senses—even by torture. This alarms them. Trog has gone underground, so to speak, in an attempt to hide from the matron mothers."

Sirot returned to the edge of the bed. "You've missed all of this, haven't you?" He looked at Esar-Haden. "Have you any idea how long you've been chained to a wall?"

"Time," said Esar-Haden, "behaves a little funny in a lightless cell."

"Would you like to know?"

Esar-Haden lowered his arms.

"Three years, give or take a few months," announced Sirot. He studied Esar-Haden's face, awaiting what emotions came. "Tell me your thoughts."

"My first thought was, is that all? I would have sworn it had been a dozen years if it had been one. Then," he frowned, "I thought of a lover, one whom I believed would have either bought my freedom or who would have broken me out of there, she's certainly capable of it."

"And yet she did nothing? She let you rot?"

"Seems that way," said Esar-Haden.

"Perhaps she was killed. You know how females are, always stabbing each other in the backs. Tell me her name, I'll enquire."

Esar-Haden shook his head. "I'll find out on my own." He looked at Sirot. "If you let me leave."

Sirot smiled. "Solve my little problem. Not only shall you be free, you shall be adorned with riches beyond your imagining."

Esar-Haden sighed. "Well, let me hear it."

. . .

"As is often the case, the problem is—the neighbors," said Sirot, one chubby arm around Esar-Haden's slender waist. Sirot grasped the front door and flung it open. The guard standing at the bottom of the steps glanced over his shoulder, took in the pair, then looked back out into the streets. Sirot nodded toward the wooden house across the way.

"Muscling in on your business?" Esar-Haden looked at Sirot. "No, you wouldn't need me for that. You've got them." He nodded to the guard below. "Must be something more—delicate."

"Astute as ever," said Sirot. He looked down to the guard. "Is she home?"

The guard spoke over his shoulder. "Went out with a group."

"Female troubles? You?"

"Hush, Esar. All of us males have female troubles. The 'she' in question is the daughter of a prominent house, one the big ones. Ruled by a matron mother that is to be feared. I hoped we would catch a glimpse of her, the daughter, not the mother, mind you.

"Well, this daughter is hopelessly addicted to trog. She began her career here. I was happy to have her. She spilled gold from her pockets with every step. Behavior like that is difficult to hide. Her mother found out and several warm-hearted gentlemen arrived to scoop the daughter up and take her home. I was told in not so polite terms that if I sold to her again I would find my head relocated into my—" At this Sirot shrugged his shoulders.

"You're lucky to have received a slap on the wrist."

"Indeed, but you see, discretion was the word that day. Our little lush was dried out, as they say, only it didn't stick. She was back with the new moon." Sirot laughed, as the moon could not be seen from Pwyll. "She was displeased to find my hospitality and my trog denied her.

"As you know, an addict finds a way. Her solution? To buy the property next door and turn it into a party house. This I can accept, the Ghetto of White Skin is filled to bursting with such places. Furthermore, she buys massive quantities of trog from my competition and gives it away, attracting a colorful assortment ranging from the highest to the lowest."

Sirot held up a pudgy finger. "This too, I overlook. I have found that such arrangements tend to implode." He lowered his finger and frowned. "Unfortunately there is another element to all of this. Her Matron Mother is losing face. Word is spreading about her daughter's excesses. What will she do? Scoop up her daughter? Dry her out? That has failed already. Kill her daughter to save the reputation of the house? That too is defeat. If the Matron Mother is forced to slay her own daughter because she cannot control her, how can she be expected to keep the discipline of her house army? How long before one of her rivals senses weakness?" Sirot shook his head. "This situation doesn't bode well for us."

"You," said Esar-Haden.

"Us, need I remind you who owns you now?" asked Sirot. "The Matron Mother in question sees a way to kill two birds with one stone. She is contemplating sending her soldiers down here to destroy both my house and hers." He nodded across the street. "These soldiers will smuggle the daughter back home under the cover of warfare. They will of course kill me. Then, the Matron Mother will vilify me, paint me as a sinister pusher of an addictive drug."

"Aren't you?"

"Yes, but that's beside the point. The Matron Mother will say to her peers, 'he had corrupted my daughter, yes, but do you find your daughters free from his influence? I've done all of us the favor of getting rid of him. I've gone further and soon the Skin will be rid of all like him. Trog will be banished from Pwyll forever. I am the only Matron Mother ruthless enough to do this.'"

"Don't tell me you want *her* killed?" asked Esar-Haden, raising an eyebrow at Sirot. "Not even I can assassinate a Matron Mother like her."

Sirot smiled. "The mother, no." He turned and looked across the street. "The daughter, yes."

Esar-Haden contemplated the situation. He looked at Sirot, then looked across the street. Something, he realized, didn't add up. When it came to him, he smiled. "Which house is backing you?"

Sirot narrowed his eyes. "I pride myself on—"

"Stop it," interrupted Esar-Haden. "I've counted a half dozen guards. Maybe you've got a dozen, fresh from academy. The Matron Mother could have relocated your head already, and would have," Esar studied Sirot, "unless you've got a house behind you she isn't so quick to anger."

Sirot pulled Esar-Haden out of the doorway and shut the door. "Damn you," he growled. "In front of the help!"

"That's why you sprung me. You can't send your men over there to bash her skull in. It would mean war between the two houses." Esar-Haden laughed. "You figured you would resurrect the dead. Send a forgotten man over there to slice her up. I'm sure when you bought my freedom you also paid for my jailers to forget not only your name but mine. 'Esar-Haden? Never heard of him.'"

Sirot smiled. "Smart plan, eh?"

"Cute, except there's one problem."

"Don't think you're up to it?"

Esar-Haden frowned. "The problem is, once the deed is done you've got to put my name out there, give the Matron Mother someone to kill, otherwise it's still you."

"Esar, I'm hurt. I wouldn't! The plan is to make you rich. What you do from there is your own concern. I figured you would relish a trip above, after all, you've been below for such a long time." Sirot almost managed to sound magnanimous.

Esar-Haden looked to the closed door, seeing instead the party house on the other side. "Killing her is easy." He looked at Sirot, "Getting away is the hard part." He frowned. "I'd like to go back to my cell now."

Sirot played the part of the wounded man. "Esar, really? I expected more from you. You've the kind of exploits that bards make songs of. This should be no problem for you." He squeezed Esar-Haden's waist and began to direct him deeper into the house. "I know that you don't trust me. I don't blame you. Despite this, it's my hope that we shall become dear friends. I've restored you to life! I'll restore you still further. All you have to do is, as you say, 'slice up' a pesky daughter of a powerful house. Why, I think you would jump at the chance, given what they've done to you."

"It's the exit strategy, Sirot."

"That can be arranged."

"I'm sure it already has."

"Ye of little faith!" cried Sirot. "Us males must stick together, otherwise we'll never get ahead."

"What's to keep me from splitting?"

"Meaning?"

"Unless you're going to have your men beside me the whole time, which we've already established you can't, what's to stop me from vanishing once I'm out of your sight?"

Sirot stopped, withdrew his arm, and stepped around to face Esar-Haden. He rubbed his palms together. "Oh, I was hoping you'd ask," he said, grinning. "I do love an elaborate plan. You see, I thought of that myself, how to keep you on task."

"And?" asked Esar-Haden.

"Oh, it's almost painful to spill my secret but I see now I've no choice. Yes, you've guessed right, there is a powerful entity behind me, but it's not at all a noble house. Any guesses what it is?"

"How would I know?"

"Oh, the clues, the clues, Esar! They're all around you."

"You're being an asshole."

"Oh, fine, take the fun out of it. Are you aware of the secret wizard's enclave out there in the tunnels and forgotten caverns outside of Pwyll?"

"One hears rumors."

"While they are renegade males, some having fled their houses, some living double lives, when they all come together they are not only as powerful as any house, they are twice as deadly, for they aren't burdened by infighting. They aren't constantly looking over their shoulders, thus all of their considerable potency can be pointed at the enemy." Sirot stepped close to Esar-Haden and spoke in a conspiratorial whisper. "It's they who discovered trog. Do you know how the drug came about its name?"

"I was thinking it sounded stupid," observed Esar-Haden.

"One of their number discovered that when a troglodyte, you know, one of those disgusting frogmen we so often find scurrying around in our tunnels, is, well, in a situation of extreme distress, it secretes a mucus from glands in its throat. This mucus exits through slits not unlike gills, coating the skin. This mucus can be collected and allowed to crystalize."

"That's trog? Troglodyte slime?"

"It forms the foundation. Certain refinements are made, but at bottom, yes, troglodyte slime."

"So somewhere there are a bunch of troglodytes being tortured for their mucus?"

Sirot smiled.

"What does this have to do with me?"

"The enclave has a vested interest in my business. This isn't just drug dealing, it's insurrection. There are larger objectives than profit. They know all about you, Esar-Haden. They know all about what you're going to do to help the cause. So, as you can imagine, they're keeping an eye on you; crystal balls, scrying pools, and all that. Should you make a run for it," Sirot giggled, "who knows what magic might follow."

"Then why not just have them blast the girl?"

"Here your imagination fails you, Esar," said Sirot. "If getting at a daughter of a powerful house were so easy then bolts of lightning and disintegrating rays would be a common occurrence in Pwyll. No, such tactics are taken into account and countered in advance. The daughters of the most powerful houses are laden down with scarabs of protection, counter-spelling magics, and so on. They have the resources others lack."

"Including me," said Esar-Haden.

"Such is the way of things."

"You could be bluffing."

"Call it."

Esar-Haden sighed. "What's her name?"

"Vayla Koss," said Sirot. He studied Esar-Haden's face. "What? What is it? No!" He laughed, realizing. "It can't be—is she? Oh, Esar-Haden is she? Ha! She is!" Sirot's stomach shook as he laughed.

. . .

Esar-Haden managed to dart between her bodyguards and touch her elbow. He was grabbed, his arms pinned behind his back, a dagger at his throat, but he eked out, "I thought I would have seen you sooner, Vayla."

She turned her head, surprised at being touched or even addressed by an unknown male. She stayed the hand of his would be killer. "Esar-Haden?" She laughed. "Where have you been hiding?" She leaned into him, put her arms around his neck, and whispered into his ear. "Come with me. I'm on my own now, I can have any man I please. Even the lowliest cockroach in the Skin can share my bed." She laughed, taking joy in her excess.

He said nothing.

She disentangled herself from him, studied him. "No, not you," she said. "Not anymore. We've had our fun, haven't we, Esar?"

"I thought it was more than mere fun."

She glanced at her bodyguards, "Let him go," she commanded. They threw him to the ground. She looked down at him. She seemed on the verge of speech, as memories and feelings were flooding over her, but turned and walked away instead.

Esar-Haden rolled onto his side, propped himself up on his elbow, and watched his former lover and her entourage disappear into the crowded streets of the Skin.

"Let's recap," he mumbled to himself. "Sirot wants me to kill the woman I love but who left me to rot. The brotherhood of renegade males will kill me if I try to leave town. Matron Mother Prim Koss will flay me alive if I assassinate her daughter." He stood and dusted himself off. "Well, Esar, how do you get out of this without dying?"

. . .

Esar-Haden knocked on the gate. He could feel eyes on him, unseen eyes, behind unseen weapons. He reached up and knocked again. He hummed a tune to himself. He stopped humming when a clanking sound came from behind the gate. A smaller door within the larger gate opened and an angry looking female stepped out. Half a dozen males rushed out from behind her, surrounding Esar-Haden, weapons in hand. The female looked him over.

"What do you want, male?" she spat at him.

"I'm here to see Matron Mother Prim Koss."

The female did not changer her expression. The males surrounding him remained silent. Long seconds passed. The female looked over Esar-Haden's shoulder. Something hard struck him in the back of the head. When he woke up he was naked, shackled to something meant to stretch him until his bones came out of their joints. An aged, impatient-looking dark elf female was standing over to him.

"Matron Mother?" asked Esar-Haden.

The Matron Mother of House Koss looked down at him, her face communicating her extreme annoyance.

. . .

Esar-Haden knocked a third time on a door belonging to House Koss—Vayla's. A male opened the door and fell into his arms.

"Oops," he said, giggling.

Esar-Haden smelled drink on him. He set him up on his feet.

"I know you," said the male, poking Esar-Haden in the chest. "Didn't we kick dirt in your face the other day?" He giggled. "You back for more?"

"I've come to make amends," said Esar-Haden.

"Make what?" asked the male, swaying.

"Vayla Koss, you remember her, right?"

"Uh-huh."

"I'm here to lay on my belly and beg for her forgiveness."

"I would like to see that," said the male, swinging open the door.

. . .

"He sent *you*?" asked Vayla Koss. She was lying in an enormous bed, fully nude, her skin glistening with recent exertion. A nude female, young, lithe, and supremely attractive reposed on one side of her, a male, thin, bald-headed, with glowing runes carved into his bare chest stretched and yawned on the other.

"On the surface they call it an olive branch," said Esar-Haden.

"A what?" asked Vayla.

"It means a peace offering. Sirot knows that the trog you've been getting from his competitors is not of the quality you've come to expect—that you deserve."

"Go on," said Vayla.

"Sirot feels his earlier behavior was misguided. He relishes the opportunity to make it up to you."

"How would he do that?" asked Vayla.

"He wishes to throw a party in your honor."

"A party?" scoffed Vayla. "I party here every night. I don't need him anymore."

26

Esar-Haden looked over the other occupants of the bed. He glanced around the room. He returned his eyes to Vayla. "It gets old, doesn't it? I know. I've done all this, lived this life, minus the trog but with plenty of booze. Each party must outdo the one previous. It keeps escalating. Before you know it you're considering human sacrifice just to stifle the yawns."

Vayla smirked. "Maybe you were doing it wrong, Esar."

"You look bored, Vayla. You never looked bored with me."

"I never was, but you disappeared. What's a girl to do?"

"Find out why."

Vayla scoffed at him. "Me chase after you? I'm the daughter of a powerful house. Who are you? A nobody, a male, a—"

"I was your lover," interjected Esar-Haden, "not like these two, or the hundreds you've had since me. We were in love."

Vayla looked at the rune-chested male, "get out." She turned to the girl on the other side. "Both of you." They rose, gathered what clothing they could find, and fled the room. Esar-Haden noted that the pair of guards standing just inside the door remained. Vayla got out bed and went to a porcelain basin. She grabbed a towel, wetted it, and began to bathe herself. Her back was to him, but she looked at his reflection in the mirror above the basin. "Why didn't they execute you?"

"So you knew?"

She locked eyes with him through the mirror. "You just couldn't play by the rules, could you, Esar? You had to go and make enemies. You couldn't control yourself." She spun, water flying from her, sparkling in the dim glow of the magical orbs of light floating about the room. "What was I supposed to do? Buy your freedom?"

"Yeah," said Esar.

"Oh, is that right? And what would my mother have thought of that?"

"Probably something more charitable than her thoughts are about all of this," said Esar-Haden, waving his arm to indicate the room, her current way of life, and her addiction to trog.

Vayla turned back to the basin and looked in the mirror. "I had to forget you. I had to imagine you as already dead. Yet here you are."

"Here I am."

"Why? For Sirot? To regain my business? Is that why you're here?"

"I'm here for a lot of reasons, that's one of them."

"What are the others?"

Esar-Haden sat on the edge of the bed. He reached down and smoothed out the sheet. "I wonder if we can't regain what was lost."

Vayla laughed. "Really, Esar?"

Esar looked up at her reflection in the mirror. He didn't like the look on her face and turned away. "There's a new strain," he glanced at her, "of trog. More powerful, lasts longer, and—"

She spun to face him. "And what?"

"A new technique," he said, "Sirot figured it out."

"Meaning?"

He looked at her. "You can decide ahead of time where to go. No more hoping for the best. You want to flutter around with angels in Elysium? Dance with the Fae in Arcadia? Brandish a red-hot poker in the torture chambers of Hell? Whatever you want, *wherever* you want."

Vayla crossed the room and stood close to him. "Are you serious?"

He looked up at her. "Interested?"

"Of course!"

Esar-Haden stood. The guards stepped forward, their hands on the hilts of their swords. Esar-Haden ignored them. "Tomorrow night. You know the place." He took a step toward the door, but stopped and spoke over his shoulder. "Bring all your friends. Sirot's got plenty of trog. Remember, you're the guest of honor." He looked into her eyes, "better think about where you want to go."

. . .

"Are you insane?" asked Sirot.

"You hired me to solve your problem."

"This isn't a solution! It's the very thing I'm trying to avoid! Besides, what you told her can't even be done. How could you make that up? What am I supposed to tell her when she—"

"It won't go that far."

"Because she'll kill me!"

Esar-Haden shrugged his shoulders. "Take it or leave it."

"Leave it!"

"Then I fight my way out of here, try to flee Pwyll, and test the magical aptitude of your brotherhood of pissed-off males."

Sirot stared at him in disbelief. "You *are* insane!"

. . .

"Vayla!" cried Sirot as if being reunited with a long lost friend. He rounded the table, rushed to her as quickly as his bulk allowed, took her hand in his and began to kiss her fingers.

Vayla, for her part, was disdainful and aloof, encouraging further debased groveling from Sirot. Her friends swarmed into the room as if they were hellbent on destroying it. They knocked aside Sirot's armed guards as if handling human filth from the surface.

Esar-Haden sat on the edge of the table, taking in the scene. Vayla, he thought, looked as ravishing as ever. She was tall, athletic, yet not overly muscular, and possessed the kind of seductive arrogance only the daughter of a powerful house was able to own. Even though he had cursed her and had sworn vengeance should he somehow escape death at the hands of the executioner, even though he had prayed to every demon he could name to strike her down, or afflict her with a wasting disease, or to consume her soul, he realized he still loved her.

Her eyes flashed when they met his. The corners of her mouth began to turn upwards but she forced a frown and looked away.

"Sirot?"

"Yes, Vayla?" asked Sirot, looking up but still kissing her fingers.

"Why do you hate me?"

Sirot stood and placed his pudgy hands over his heart. "Hate?" He shook his head. "My dear Vayla. I was —" He lowered his gaze. She looked down at him.

"Yes?"

"A fool. Forgive me."

Vayla looked over the room. Her eyes once more fell on Esar-Haden. She studied him. "Esar tells me you've," she looked at Sirot, "discovered a new technique?"

A smile spread over Sirot's face. "Where would you like to go, Mistress?"

Vayla smiled. She threw her long, toned arms over Sirot's shoulders. "First, feed me, pour the best wines down my throat." She laughed, reached down, and patted

Sirot's protruding midsection. "You always have the best, Sirot."

"I've put together a feast fit for a queen." Sirot smiled. "I've procured the best brandy, cognac, and champagne available anywhere, all for you, Vayla."

"I love how you spoil me," said Vayla, pulling Sirot toward the table. She passed Esar-Haden, reached out, and drug her hand across his jaw. "To the kitchen, male. Fetch me a bottle of champagne."

"Anything you wish, Mistress," said Esar-Haden.

The kitchen was packed with males rushing to put the finishing touches on the hors d' oeuvres: rissoles chateaubriand, amandes salées, and seasoned olives. Esar-Haden paused, picked up one of the olives and popped it into his mouth. He grabbed a bottle of champagne, took a swig, then began to set it back but kept it instead. He went to the back door, opened it and stepped out. When he did not return Sirot used his disappearance to excuse himself.

Esar-Haden was half way down the block when Matron Mother Prim Koss rounded the corner, leading a small army of males. Two of her other daughters walked with her. The others would be at the house, with the bulk of her army, just in case. The Ghetto of White Skin had come to a standstill at the arrival of such a powerful Matron Mother. Esar-Haden stepped to the side of the avenue and bowed his head. Others were quick to join him.

At about the same moment that Matron Mother Koss passed, Sirot wedged his way in beside Esar-Haden. He bowed his head and remained silent. Although Prim Koss knew who the two males were she ignored them. Once her and her daughters had passed Esar-Haden heard Sirot whisper aloud, "Unbelievable."

Esar and Sirot looked up at the same moment. "How did you do it?" asked Sirot.

Esar-Haden turned and looked at him. He looked past him to watch Matron Mother Prim Koss climb the steps and enter the drug den. He felt bad for Vayla. He was certain it would be awhile before he saw her again. She might even end up chained to a wall and he knew how unpleasant that was. He watched as the soldiers of House Koss surrounded the building and began yanking out Vayla's friends and hanger-ons. He felt bad for them, knowing the majority of them hadn't long to live.

"Esar?"

He looked at Sirot.

"Are you certain?"

Esar-Haden reached into his pocket and produced the key to the party house that Vayla Koss no longer had need of. "She's going to tear down your house of ill repute. She needs something theatrical." Esar-Haden dropped the key into Sirot's open palm. Sirot gazed at it in amazement. "You can set up business across the street—in a few weeks." Sirot looked at Esar-Haden. "Prim gets thirty percent."

Sirot looked down the avenue. "Now I have two powerful backers." He looked at Esar-Haden and shook his head in disbelief. He looked back at his former place of business with a wistful smile. "I'll miss the old joint."

Esar-Haden threw one arm over Sirot's shoulders and offered him the bottle.

"Now, about those vast riches you're going to laden me down with."

Hashishin

Prince Khurram felt the roughness of the stone floor against his knees, the chill against his palms. The air he breathed was devoid of moisture. He kissed the hem of the old man's robe. The bright colors of the fabric beneath his lips, the brilliance of the gems, and the pattern of the brocade were all lost in the gloom of his prison cell. Prince Khurram held this obsequious pose and waited.

The old man waited too, for the span of three breaths, then spoke. "Rise."

Khurram sat back, his legs under him, and looked up into the old man's bearded face. "The Old Man of the Mountain," he whispered so that the guard on the other side of his cell door would not hear. Not that the old man feared the guard—or anyone.

His was a powerful face: broad forehead, sculpted nose, and a strong jaw shaping his short, white beard. His white hair was a lion's mane. The musculature of his physique was visible even beneath the many folds of his near-priceless robe of rare silks and gems.

"Unburden your heart," said the old man.

He had come to the prison cell under the guise of a cleric, to absolve the prince of his sins. Both men knew that the ruse must work, for Prince Khurram was allowed no visitors but the gods, upon pain of death.

Prince Khurram was the heir apparent. His father, Jahangir, was the emperor. His father was not a war-like man, as Akbar had been. It was Akbar that had conquered the warrior-princes and unified the land. The ruthless old soldier had built an empire, then died. Now his son, a man who sat upon soft cushions, a man of wine, women, and poetry, ruled it. Jahangir, knowing he did not fill the shoes left for him, had a fragile ego and a quick temper. He

33

sentenced those who slighted him—man or woman—to endless tortures, relieved only by death. Now he was dying.

His own brother had already succumbed to royal excess. Jahangir was soon to follow. A man with a weak constitution can drink only so much wine and bed so many maidens before his heart fails him.

Khurram had made the mistake of ambition. He knew his father was weak and began to maneuver for the throne. To reward his impatience, the Emperor imprisoned him. Jahangir did not disown his eldest son nor did he take away the promise of the throne. He was only humbling his son, it was supposed. Yet Khurram worried that his father, his mind addled by wine, had forgotten him.

Khurram's mother was the Emperor's first wife. Jahangir had taken three other wives. It was politics-by-matrimony. The warrior-princes would not stay subdued. In order to placate them, Jahangir married their daughters, bringing them into the royal household. Unsurprisingly, one of these wives seduced him and had been scheming for years to seize the throne.

Much to her chagrin she had not given birth to a son, only daughters. Undaunted, she married the most beautiful of these daughters to Khurram's eldest son. Sensing her husband's approaching demise, the Empress, along with the warrior-princes—who saw a way to return to power—backed Janghir's grandson, a mere boy, to be emperor. If his son were to ascend to the throne, Khurram knew his own death would follow.

"I nurture sin and fear in my heart," said Khurram. He rose and turned in order to gaze out of the solitary window of his cell. In the distance, and over the tops of the roofs of the intervening buildings—for his was a tower cell —he could just make out the distant mountains. "The sun sets behind those mountains," he said. "How magnificent must the setting sun look from those peaks." He turned and gazed at the old man. "How deep must its shadows be in those valleys."

The Old Man of the Mountain resumed his seat in the cell's only chair. "You nurture—"

"My son is innocent," said Khurram, looking at the old man. He turned back to his view, watching as the last rays of the sun set the mountain peaks aflame. "I fear for him. Such innocence," he gazed over his shoulder at the old man, "is precious." He returned his gaze to the mountains. "Once lost, it can never be regained. I fear that my son will become tainted, ruined by," he looked at the old man, "power."

"You fear for his soul?"

"There is little time left to prevent disaster. I have heard rumors, even in here, that my mother-in-law prefers that my son becomes emperor. As we both know, my father long ago designated that role to me. I do not jealously crave power. I do not strive for the throne. I gave up that dream." He looked around his cell. "This is what I deserve." He returned his gaze to the old man. "But my son, what does *he* deserve? He, so innocent, so pure, would he be—degraded—by the throne? What does *she* want for him, my mother-in-law? A wife? A harem? Fawning courtiers? Poetry? The sweet wines that my father kills himself with?"

"Do you fear he will be barred from Heaven?"

"You understand."

The Old Man of the Mountain nodded.

"My heart is heavy," continued Prince Khurram. "I have sinned enough to condemn myself to Hell."

"The gods are ready to forgive—"

"I do not wish it." Khurram shook his head. "I am full of sin." He looked at the old man. "Only a man whose heart is as black as mine can succeed as emperor. A heart free of sin, a heart made of light, does not belong on this plane of filth. Such a heart belongs in Heaven, with the gods and their perfect creations."

"Send your son to Heaven?"

"Will you? Can you? To save him."

The Old Man of the Mountain rose. He locked eyes with Prince Khurram for the span of three breaths, then nodded.

· · ·

A young man had been sent to gather a bolt of fine silk for Esar-Haden. The dark elf rogue and adventurer was being treated to round-after-round of drinks at the street cafe, even though it had been closed for hours. The proprietor was half-asleep at another table, having put up all the chairs but the one in which he slumped and those belonging to his guests. He had not stayed open out of kindness or greed but because these men were dangerous and to be respected. The young man called to announce his return.

"Ah, here," said Rafiq, pulling the youth near. "Our kingdom's finest silk," he said. "This pattern was invented by the Sultan's personal tailor. We broke into his shop three weeks ago." He offered the silk. "A gift to you, our most revered guest."

Esar-Haden set the ceramic cup down and took the cloth in his hands. He was from Pwyll, a subterranean city of dark elves who lived by raiding caravans and by forcing slaves to mine ores for trade. He, like every citizen of Pwyll, was a good judge of materials. He rubbed the silk between the tips of his fingers and knew that Rafiq was telling the truth.

"My cousin," said Waqaar. Esar-Haden turned and looked into the speaker's face. "Is a tailor, quite skilled. He can make anything you like." Waqaar nodded to the fabric.

"It would be my honor if you allow me to pay. A pleasure!"

"Gentlemen," said Esar, smiling, "friends. Why do I deserve this honor?" Even though he asked, Esar knew the answer. He was amongst his own kind: men who lived by their wits and by the quickness of their sword arms, who laughed at death, and who had no care for tomorrow.

The gathering of men shared knowing looks amongst each other. Dark elves were rare in their kingdom, but their reputation was known. To have such a quasi-mythical figure amongst them acted as an intoxicant. To learn that this visitor from distant lands was like themselves filled them with a sense of camaraderie, as if one of their own had returned after being feared lost.

"Tell us another story," said Rafiq. "Tell us of your people." He smiled, revealing a gold tooth, and looked at his fellows then back to Esar-Haden. "Tell us of your *women*." The men laughed. They expected the dark elf to laugh with them and when he didn't they were quick to prod him toward less offensive subject matter.

"You want to know about dark elf women?" he asked, an edge to his voice.

"No, no, not that," said Rafiq. "Tell us of treasure, gold and jewels, tell us of the wealth you have won and lost—"

Esar-Haden looked at Rafiq. The deep luster of his eyes—the emotion within—silenced him. The men were relieved when Esar-Haden smiled. He picked up his cup, downed the last of its contents and sat back. "I'll tell you about our women." He looked into every man's face, then stared off, remembering.

"When I was in the military academy," he looked at Rafiq, "only us males went to the academy—not by choice." He again looked into the past. "Occasionally a group of females used to come to torment us. You must know that our culture is ruled by two things: fear and sex. Our women control both. Well, this little clique of females got the grand idea to force themselves onto us. They would come when they pleased and demand that us cadets put on a show. Our instructors hated it, but what could they do?"

He reached for his cup but paused, knowing it to be empty. Waqaar poured the contents of his own cup into Esar-Haden's. Esar smiled, lifted the cup, nodded to Waqaar, then drank. He set the cup down and continued.

"These females wanted to torture and degrade us. Such things excite them." He shrugged his shoulders. "But they didn't want to do it themselves. We, being males and worse, being cadets, were beneath them. The solution? Have us torture each other. Oh, they said something quite different. They said they were checking on our training, something about their civic duty. They wanted a mock battle—but we knew.

"We knew what they really wanted: flesh torn, blood spouting in great jets, cries of anguish, the trembling hands of fear." Esar-Haden smiled. "What could we do? We fought each other, beating each other with wooden swords until we collapsed in pain and fatigue. After their show these females went home and demanded their pleasure slaves—," he chuckled, knowing the men would know what came next. "We were foreplay." He shook his head.

"They wanted more. Well, after the third time they'd come to torture us we knew we had to figure something out. Now, luckily, we had a few practice swords made out of reeds. They didn't break bones or leave bruises—as our wooden swords did—but with each hit they gave a loud *snap* and sliced open flesh.

"The next time this little clique of sadistic hedonist demanded a mock battle we were ready. We stripped down to our shorts—having always done so for them—

and began our fight, only, we used the reed swords. The females took to the *snap* of them with obvious pleasure. The blood intoxicated them. To this we added our own bit of melodrama. We got good at moving with a hit but making it appear that we had suffered a terrible blow. We became experts at mimicking the desperate howling of broken men. In short, we became actors." The men laughed.

"Our new tactics had an immediate effect. Our audience couldn't last until we were finished. They threw their skirts aside and—" He held out his hands, indicating the rest could be imagined. The men laughed at this. Their laughter woke the proprietor. Waqaar rose, went to cafe owner, and demanded more wine.

"Are they all like that?" asked Rafiq.

"Every single one," said Esar-Haden.

"It is as we feared," said Rafiq. "Your race is corrupt beyond the power of redemption."

"Well," said Esar-Haden, smiling, "is that such a bad thing?"

Waqaar returned and they all drank to corruption.

. . .

Esar-Haden was awoken by the soft touch of fawning females. He heard their giggles and whispered secrets. He felt the heat of their hands on him, of their bodies hovering over his. For a moment he kept his eyes closed. He was able to fool himself into believing he was dreaming. Yet, being a dark elf, having been raised in Pwyll, where danger is a constant, he could not stay relaxed.

He opened his eyes. He was on his stomach. He was lying on a low bed in an outdoor pavilion. He was in the shade but sunlight filtered in, partially blinding him. The sweet aroma of fragrant flowers filled his nostrils. Their colors wavered before his eyes. He heard the layered songs of many birds, all singing to one another in peace and harmony. Somewhere near a spring gurgled. And again the females giggles.

Esar-Haden spun onto his back. He lifted his head and saw two women bent over him. He grabbed the nearest wrist and looked, for he feared a dagger. But the woman's hand was empty. He looked now at the pair.

The owner of the wrist was a woman in her late twenties, if he had to guess her age. Her skin was tanned, her eyes dark, her face diamond-shaped. Her black hair cascaded over her bare shoulders. She wore a pair of chunky gold earrings in the shape of cobras. A thin chain of gold around her slender neck held the same charm. From the tail of the cobra extended a thread of purple silk. This purple line snaked between her breasts, for other than jewelry, she wore only dappled sunlight.

Esar-Haden looked at the other girl. Her skin was bronzed. Her hair only a shade darker than her skin. Her eyes were sparkling blue. Her full lips were wine-red. She batted her long eyes lashes and smiled at Esar-Haden. Her teeth were perfectly-shaped and white. Unlike the other woman she wore a top that covered her small breasts. It was blue and had a pattern of interlocking circles. The girl's shoulders and mid-rift were bare.

Esar-Haden felt the tug of the woman's wrist. He held her fast, turning to look at her. He felt a warm breeze and realized he was nude. He instinctively reached to where his daggers would have hung and felt only his hip bone.

"Do you fear?" asked the woman whose wrist he held. The other girl said something in a language Esar-Haden could not understand, then giggled. She resumed massaging him, running her hands along his thighs.

"Do you not recognize where you are?" asked the woman. Esar-Haden looked all around him. He saw no immediate signs of danger. He turned back to the woman and released her wrist. She sat back and resumed massaging his chest, arms, and shoulders. "You're in Heaven."

"Not me," he said, "I don't deserve Heaven. I should be in Hell."

The brunette laughed. "Hell? Why, Esar-Haden? Why should you be in Hell?"

"How do you know my name?"

The brunette smiled but remained mute.

"All dark elves end up in Hell," he said. The brunette glanced at him, their eyes locking. "As if my race weren't enough to purchase entry to the fiery abode," Esar smiled, "I've sinned."

"Sin?" asked the brunette. She looked at the girl and spoke in the language they shared that Esar-Haden did not. The girl giggled again. The brunette looked back at Esar. "There is no such thing as sin. There is only pleasure and displeasure. Here," she looked around her, "there is only pleasure."

"Where is 'here'?"

"I told you." She looked at the girl and spoke again. The girl smiled, then stood. A long, colorful wrap was tied around her waist. She untied it, revealing her smooth sex.

"You are in Heaven, Esar-Haden," said the brunette. "Here there is only pleasure."

. . .

Esar-Haden again awoke with a sense of displacement. He smelled sweet perfumes and remembered that he had spent all afternoon with the two women. He must have fallen asleep in their arms.

He rose on his elbow and looked around him. He was still in the outdoor pavilion. He could see now that the pavilion and surrounding garden were sunk deep in a mountain valley. The sun was setting behind a nearby peak, crowning it in gold. He sat up and stretched. He pulled a sheet over his nakedness. He was, as far as he could tell, alone.

He rose, wrapping the sheet around him, and went to the edge of the pavilion. He saw movement and for a moment was alarmed but it was only a large bird that he had stirred from slumber. The bird rose and extended its fantastic plumage, then strutted away.

"Does my garden please you?" called a deep, masculine voice.

Esar-Haden spun. Standing at the other end of the pavilion was a broad-shouldered, white-bearded man in a simple robe of muslin. A quick glance alerted Esar-Haden that the man was unarmed, but he also observed that the man, despite his age, was physically strong. The man stepped forward.

"How did you find the company of my daughters?"

"Daughters?" asked Esar-Haden.

"I have many daughters," said the old man. "You will know them all."

"Where am I? Why have you brought me here? How —"

"Did my daughter not tell you?" asked the old man. He smiled. "Yes, she told you. And my other daughter, did she not *show* you?"

"Heaven?" asked Esar-Haden. He shook his head.

"Come," said the man, waving. He turned and left the pavilion.

"My armor and daggers?" asked Esar-Haden. "I'm not going anywhere until—"

The old man turned. "There is no displeasure here. Come."

Esar-Haden, the sheet still held around him, followed. The old man led him down a winding, stone path that wove its way through the dense cluster of flowering bushes and trees. He stopped before a sheer face of rock.

Much of it was hidden by foliage. In the rock were a trio of natural bowls. One was filled with wine, another with milk, another with pure water. The old man felt along the rock and found a goblet sitting on a natural shelf. He dipped it into the wine, lifted it to his lips, and drank. He refilled the cup and handed it to Esar-Haden.

Esar studied the three natural bowls. He saw ripples in the wine, milk, and water. It was apparent that the bowls were filled from within the rock, as if the mountain itself delivered the mana of the gods.

"You shall want for nothing," said the old man. "My daughters shall serve you. If you want wine," he motioned, "the stone itself shall provide." He waved his hand. "Every form of beauty is here, all the treasures of nature are here. Song, dance, love making—there is only pleasure to be had." He looked at Esar-Haden, "All this is yours."

"Why do I deserve this honor?" asked Esar-Haden.

The old man smiled and passed Esar-Haden, intent on returning to the pavilion. Esar-Haden followed. The old man crossed to the other side of the pavilion and stood looking up at the moon, for the sun had set. He studied the silver light as it illuminated the mountain peaks. Esar-Haden stood near the bed, holding the goblet of wine.

"A certain kind of man knows of," he paused, "the *greatest* possible pleasures." He turned and looked at Esar-Haden. "You are such a man."

"Am I?"

"Yes."

"What kind of pleasures?"

"A legendary warrior once said, 'The greatest joy a man can know is to conquer his enemies and drive them before him; to ride their horses and take away their

43

possessions; to see the faces of those who were dear to them wet with tears; and to clasp their wives and daughters in his arms.'" He paused. "Such pleasure—"

"Cannot be had here," finished Esar-Haden.

The old man shook his head. "This," he held out his hands, indicating the mountain valley and all within, "is the reward promised to man by the gods. I give this reward to you, Esar-Haden, and all I ask is that you experience those other kinds of pleasures."

"I have no enemies."

"Nor I, but men have enemies—and wants. There is a certain man that has an enemy and wants him killed."

"So kill him."

"Such an act is beneath a god."

"A god?"

"This is Heaven, is it not? I created it. My daughters are the most beautiful in the world, I created them, also. I brought you here, to my house." He nodded. "Yes, I am a god, and I cannot know those other kind of pleasure, for those are man's pleasures."

"You want me to kill?"

"To experience pleasure, Esar-Haden."

"And if I 'experience pleasure', as you say," Esar looked around, "Heaven?"

"Yes."

"Who?"

"Shahryar, Prince Khurram's son, the Emperor's grandson."

"If I refuse?"

The old man did not smile. "Why would you refuse pleasure?"

Esar-Haden sat on the low bed. "Send me two more of your daughters," he said, lifting the goblet to his lips. "And I'll think about it."

. . .

Esar-Haden again awoke feeling disoriented and anxious. His head pounded and his stomach ached. There was a familiar taste on his tongue but it wasn't wine, food, or women. It was an herb he knew well. That he had ingested it was what made him ill, for he was in the habit of smoking the dried herb.

He was no longer on the low bed in the pavilion but had somehow returned to the room he had rented above the cafe. He was nude and in the uncomfortable rented bed. He rolled over onto his side and saw that his armor and daggers were tossed over the room's only chair. He had covered the window with a cloth and he could tell from the light burning away at the edges, making a ragged rectangle, that it was day.

He sat up and rubbed his temples. He stood and examined himself. He was unhurt. He searched his belongings, nothing was missing—not even the small pouch of the suspected herb, for the herb he drank had not been his. He returned to the bed and sat. He leaned back against the wall and replayed everything in his mind.

. . .

Esar-Haden was approaching Shepherd's Gate. The paving stones had been scuffed by the passage of thousands of hooves and stained by urine and feces. The air smelled of beasts, hay, and sweat. The moon shone overhead, making the shadows sharp-edged. He had a premonition he was being followed and turned down an alley. He ran, turning down the crooked allies until he arrived back at Shepherd's Gate.

He studied the shadows and saw a single figure wrapped in dark fabric. He loosed the hand-crossbow from his belt, pulled a dart from his bandolier, dipped it in poison, loaded it, and aimed at the dark form. He waited, watching. Whomever it was had lost him. The figure searched the shadows, looking left and right. Esar-Haden returned his bolt and crossbow, drew one of his daggers, and began to circle around.

He got behind the figure and crept along the wall until, with a silent leap, he was able to grab her and place the knife at her throat. He yanked the scarf from her face.

"You?" It was the brunette from the pavilion. "What are you doing?"

"Watching you," she said, with no hint of fear in her voice. Esar-Haden did not lower his dagger, but kept it against her throat.

"Why?"

"My father bid me to," she said, her dark eyes like twin jets reflecting the moonlight, "just as he bid me to lay with you. I do my father's bidding—with pleasure."

Esar-Haden released her and sheathed his dagger. "Not interested." He began to turn. The brunette grabbed his arm and let him pull her from the shadows into the moonlit street.

"Would you deny yourself Heaven?"

Esar glanced over his shoulder. "I said—"

She pulled him to a stop, threw her arms around his shoulders, and kissed him. "Would you deny me? Esar— I've had you, you've had me. I *need* you. Don't you need me?"

"A suicide mission."

"For any other man, yes. For you?"

"The Emperor's grandson?" Esar-Haden shook his head. "I asked around." He nodded the direction of the palace. "A thousand armed men. A thousand servants. The harem alone contains five hundred women. You think I can sneak past all those people?"

"I do not think," said the brunette. "My father says and I do. My father says—"

"No," said Esar-Haden, throwing off her arms. She returned them.

"The garden. You must enter through the garden. It's the only way."

"I said—"

"The palace is walled but the garden goes to the river." She kissed Esar-Haden. "No wall." She reached up and caressed the golden cobra at her ear. She removed it and placed it his palm. "Slither like the snake through the Emperor's garden. Sneak past his men or kill them. The boy sleeps in a room overlooking an aspen tree, a gift from a distant people. It has no twin in the garden. Take his life, Esar, and return to me. I will satisfy your every desire. I will be your slave for eternity. I will—"

He again threw her arms from him. "No." He turned and continued toward Shepherd's Gate. She watched him, then turned and rushed the opposite direction.

. . .

Esar-Haden was not far from town when he heard rustling in the bushes beside the road. He stopped and turned. He could just see the top of Shepherd's Gate, illuminated by moonlight. He scanned the bushes. He drew his daggers and was about to use his innate magical ability to darken the area around him when someone called his name.

"Is that you?" Rafiq emerged from the bushes to gain the road. Waqaar appeared, as did a dozen others. He recognized most, but not all. They were armed and armored. Rafiq laughed. "We lay in wait and for what? To rob one of our own?" He reached out and slapped Waqaar on the shoulder. The pair approached. "Look, brother, he keeps his blades naked! Are we not friends?"

"Bag many travelers this time of night?" asked Esar-Haden. He still did not sheath his blades.

47

Rafiq narrowed his eyes. "It is true, my friend, there are few on the road at night."

"Let me pass."

"Pass?" asked Rafiq. He turned and looked down the road. "To where? There is no treasure to be had out there. There are no women, no wine. Why would you want to go out there, Esar-Haden?"

"Don't do it, Rafiq. I don't want to kill you."

"Kill?" Rafiq laughed. He walked among the dozen men. "Kill? Why, there is only one of you and—" He stopped and looked at Esar-Haden. "No, you will not kill us. It is not us you are to kill."

"What are you—" began Esar-Haden.

"There *is* one you must kill, dark elf."

"You too?"

"The Old Man of the Mountain has spoken," said Rafiq. "You must do as he commands."

"Not interested."

Rafiq looked at his men then at Esar-Haden. "He will give you Heaven, we will give you Hell."

"You didn't understand," said Esar-Haden. "You didn't listen, at the cafe, when I told you—"

"It is you who did not listen!" The men drew their weapons and began to circle around Esar-Haden. "You will kill Shahryar this night or you will die. If Heaven is not reward enough for you, we shall send you to Hell."

Esar-Haden sheathed his daggers and smiled. "Alright, Rafiq. I'll kill him."

The men were taken aback. They did not expect capitulation to come without violence. They searched one another's faces, uncertain. They looked to Rafiq, who looked at them in return before looking at Esar-Haden.

"You will?"

Esar-Haden felt the outside of a small bag that hung from his belt. He felt the gold cobra within, smiled, and nodded.

. . .

Esar-Haden crouched near the river, hidden by tall reeds. The walls went to the river's edge. The ground sloped up a hundred yards before leveling. At the top was a wide patio. Behind the patio was the palace. Between where he now crouched and the patio was a well-manicured garden.

Five armed and armored men stood at the edge of the patio, gazing down into the garden. Several other men roamed the garden, torches in hand. Whenever one of the five viewing the garden from the higher ground thought he spotted movement he would yell and point and a torch-bearing guard would rush over. Esar-Haden watched as several night-loving animals were frightened from the garden.

He glanced over his shoulder. A wide-bottomed boat was anchored in the river. A dozen men paced the deck, gripping short bows. Only his practiced stealth and his innate ability to manipulate shadow had gotten him this far. It would take skill to get him further. He couldn't help but smile.

Esar-Haden knew why Rafiq, Waqaar, and the others hadn't tried to slither like a serpent through the garden. He knew why the Old Man of the Mountain wanted him. There is an art to stealth. The mistake, he knew, that most people made was to rely on silence and slow-movement. These were components, certainly, but he knew they were secondary. The key was to move quickly when one can and to move not at all when one cannot do so without risk. The key was remaining unobserved, and sometimes remaining unobserved took quickness, boldness, and even the risk of noise.

Esar-Haden had an advantage over the guards. His eyes were matched to the darkness of night. He watched the guards. He watched where they put their attention. He watched their eyes. It was not cover alone that he sought. It was avenues of movement that would not be seen.

He rushed forward and dropped. He looked through the foliage and watched the eyes that were watching the garden. When another avenue became clear he again rushed, crouching and moving, not like a serpent, but like a scurrying rat. He fell flat on his stomach behind some flowers and again watched the eyes of the guards. He listened for their yelled alerts. When some nocturnal animal caught their attention they all looked at the same spot. He could rush ten or more yards at a time when this happened.

It took time and patience to reach the top edge of the garden. He had not been seen nor heard. He crouched at the trunk of a tree, pulled and loaded his crossbow, then fired a bolt at the wall opposite. The *tink* of the dart's tip against the stone turned every head. As the guards searched for the source of the sound, Esar-Haden slipped past them.

He was unsure what an aspen tree looked like. But he figured it would be below a window, the brunette had promised him that, and that it would be somewhat out of place, the colors darker or lighter, or something that would denote its foreignness.

He searched the garden within the walls, of which the patio was only a part. He found a tree beneath a window and, failing to find another, thought it his best guess. He scampered up the tree, leapt to the ornamental stonework surrounding the window, and peered in.

The window was open to admit the cool breeze. A single lantern was lit, giving the room a warm glow. A small table and two chairs were just beneath the window.

The lantern was on the other side of the room, on a table beside a bed. It was difficult to judge from his perch, but Esar-Haden felt there was a sole figure beneath the coverlets. He could hear a slight whistle, a sound of content sleep.

Esar-Haden looked over his shoulder. He could not see the guards, the leaves of the aspen blocked his lines of sight, nor did he hear them. He climbed into the room, passing over one of the two chairs, and crouched by the wall. There was no one in the room, other than the bed's sole occupant.

He rose and walked to the edge of the bed. A handsome boy, perhaps ten or eleven, was lying on his side, asleep. Esar-Haden pulled a single dart from the bandolier around his chest and dipped the tip into the flask of poison on his belt.

. . .

Shahryar awoke when he heard a *bang*. He looked but saw nothing. The sound was loud enough to wake him but slight enough to keep the guard posted at his door from entering.

He cleared the glue from his eyes and studied the gloom. Then he saw it, one of the chairs at his writing table was lying on its back. This puzzled him. He watched as the breeze blew the curtains and wondered if the breeze had been strong enough to knock over the chair.

Shahryar threw aside the coverlets and got out of bed. He walked to the chair and looked down at it. He looked out of the window. He lifted the chair and set it upright. He turned and went back to his bed but stopped short when he saw the note on his bedside table, a note pinned in place by a dart. He could not stop himself from emitting a startled cry. The door to his room opened and the guard stepped in.

"Prince? What is it? Are you unwell?"

Shahryar could only point.

The guard rushed over and looked at the dart and the note. For a moment he was confused and didn't know what action to take. When his wits returned, he grabbed the prince by the shoulder and hurried him from the room.

. . .

Emperor Jahangir's fourth wife (his youngest and most beautiful), who had been given first the name Nur Mahal, which meant "Light of the Palace" and who, upon giving Jahangir much pleasure, would be called Nur Jahan, "Light of the World", held her frightened soon to be son-in-law, in her arms. Although she was not his mother, she had manipulated him into loving her more than his own parents. He hardly knew his father, who had been imprisoned, nor his mother, who had been relegated to a distant room in the palace, kept from roaming free by armed guards.

Nur Jahan held the boy with one arm and held the other out to receive the note. The poison, all assumed it was poison—and it was—had been wiped free. She looked at the vizier who had handed her the note, "Magic?"

"None that I detected, Empress."

"Did you read it?"

He nodded. "To ensure no spells were hidden in the words. There are none."

Nur Jahan read the note.

In the mountains nearby, not more than a day's travel, but I do not know precisely where, lies a hidden valley. In this valley is a luxurious garden. In this garden lies a serpent who would bite you, poison you—kill you.

Nur Jahan looked at the vizier. "What does it mean?"

Before the man could respond a guard rushed in. "Forgive me," he said, bowing. "We found this."

"Approach," said Nur Jahan. The guard knelt before her, holding out his hands. "What is it?" asked Nur Jahan, leaning forward.

"A serpent of gold," said the guard.

"An earring," said the vizier, taking the serpent from the guard's hands. "You are dismissed—wait! Where did you find it?"

"Under the Prince's pillow."

. . .

The hidden stronghold of the Hashishin's was soon located. Adjacent to this stronghold was the luxurious valley, what many had called Heaven but what Esar-Haden had thought to be a nest of serpents. Emperor Jahangir's men sieged the stronghold. It took them three years but eventually the Hashishin were destroyed. The Old Man of the Mountain was the last to die. The corpse of his daughter, who wore a gold serpent on a necklace, was found and the serpents compared.

Emperor Jahangir died the following year. The impatient Shahryar, who was then fourteen, had himself declared emperor and seized the royal treasury. This angered the army, who supported Khurram.

Khurram was released and with the help of the army seized the palace, killed Shahryar, and imprisoned Nur Jahan in the cell that he had once occupied. She was allowed no slave to ease her captivity. Indeed, although she had once been empress, the guards treated her no better than the lowest prisoner.

Esar-Haden continues his adventures.

Two Daggers and a Dying Man

The Ghetto of White Skin, the most disreputable part of the subterranean dark elf city of Pwyll, erupted in battle. Esar-Haden, a boy from a poor house who spent as much time as he could in the White Skin, dove into a narrow, dead-end alley between a brothel and a theater.

"Fuck," he growled under his breath as he peeked around the corner, trying to identify the houses involved. 'Too many soldiers for this to be a pick-up fight.' When he saw a trio of armed and armored female dark elves, magic crackling down the length of their battle whips, he ducked back into the alley.

In dark elf culture, women are in charge. The daughters of important houses rarely stepped foot in the Ghetto of White Skin, called so because surface races could be found there, their skin being much lighter than the ebony skin of the dark elves. The activities that took place in that section of Pwyll were beneath them. He found the back door of a brothel, set in an alcove, and tried it. The door was locked. He pressed himself into the corner.

The sounds and smells of fighting filled the alley, echoing from the stone. The high-pitched clang of metal-on-metal, the gruesome opening of flesh, which released the alarming smell of mans' interior, the ozone scent and thundering crash of magic, the screams of men in agony all overwhelmed Esar-Haden. He banged his elbow against the door in a near panic, hoping someone would let him in, save him from certain death should he be found. He kept his eyes on the entrance to the alley. Not that he could do much if the battle came to him, he was unarmed.

A wounded soldier staggered to the entrance of the alley, collapsing against the wall. The man held a pair of daggers. He wore quilted leather armor—darkened by blood. A pair of crossbow bolts protruded from his chest. He attempted to push himself from the wall with a thrust of his shoulder but fell back against it. He staggered forward, smearing blood. The soldier managed a handful of steps before he collapsed into a seated position, his back against the stone. There he sat, his hands in his lap, the daggers fallen between his splayed legs.

The man sat motionless, head bowed. His long, blood-clumped hair hid his face. Esar subdued his fear enough to lean out of the alcove. He angled to get a better view of the daggers. "I'm no threat," said the soldier. "A prostitute," he asked, "to attend me as I die? Fitting." He was taken with a fit of coughing. "Bring me some wine, whore." The soldier lifted his head and looked directly at Esar-Haden. "Huh? A boy." He looked toward the alley's entrance. The tide of battle crested, filling the alley with dangerous echoes. The sounds soon retreated. He looked at Esar, then closed his eyes. Agony distorted his features. He squeezed his hands into fists, groaned, then relaxed. He turned his head and spit out a mixture of blood and saliva. He did not wipe his chin. He opened his eyes. "A brothel whelp? Half-elven? Son of a surface whore and a dark elf?"

"No," said Esar. "House-born." As he said this he glanced toward the mouth of the alley. The sounds of battle were less, indicating that it had moved a bit away. The soldier followed Esar-Haden's eyes.

"Won't be long." He turned back to Esar-Haden. "Ambushed 'em."

"You a soldier?" asked Esar-Haden. "What house?"

"No." The man laughed. It seemed not to pain him. "Far from it." He looked down at the wooden shafts protruding from his chest. "I'm a man who has outlived his usefulness." He looked to Esar. "I'm dying, boy."

"I can see that."

The man looked down at the bolts. "Not from these. I can't even feel—" He looked at Esar-Haden. "My back. I—" He grimaced. "Stabbed in the back." A pool of blood was forming beneath him. "I turned my back on the enemy. I ran. Adika, my eldest sister, or To-Kuta, one of them—or both—stabbed me as I passed. I deserve to die like this, with some brothel whelp watching."

"How much are those daggers worth?" asked Esar-Haden.

"Daggers?" The man frowned. The pool of blood reached the opposite wall and began to run down the slope toward Esar-Haden. The sounds of battle changed from a fight to a slaughter. "How old are you, boy?" Esar-Haden told him. This sent the man deeper into thought. Esar-Haden kept an eye on the alley's entrance. "When I was close to your age," began the man, "I went on a surface raid. My father drug me along. A ranching community had grown up a bit away from Seven Rivers, maybe two dozen families." The man's face contorted as a wave of pain moved through him. Esar-Haden elbowed the door behind him. "Boy, are you listening to me?"

"Uh huh."

"I'm trying to tell you something. We raided this little hamlet in the middle of the night. We kicked in their doors and drug them out into the moonlight, men, women, children. The livestock was huddled together, lying with their legs beneath them, sleeping, their backs glistening from dew. They looked like hairy boulders. They woke up when they heard the screaming. I remember their black eyes reflecting the moon's light. The bulls had massive horns that stuck straight out to either side, like a demon's." The man looked down at the daggers and spoke with his eyes riveted to them. "The cattle watched us as we separated the adult males from everyone else. We took them out into the scrublands, out to those tall, spare bushes, that somehow survive up there." The man looked up, toward the cave ceiling. "I remember, the men didn't fight. They didn't even try to run. They let themselves be led. That shocked me." He shook his head. "I couldn't believe it." He looked to Esar-Haden. "We made them lie face down on the desert pavement. They did it. They didn't protest, didn't fight back. They just— Then we stabbed them in the back." He frowned. "I never understood that."

"Surface men are weak."

The man looked at Esar-Haden, studied the clean, beautiful, youthful face, then looked away. "And me, stabbed in the back by my sisters? Am I weak?" Esar-Haden remained silent. The man continued, "I understand now. They weren't weak, those ranchers, they weren't cowards. Not exactly. They were," he looked to Esar-Haden, "afraid." He looked away. "It was fear that got them stabbed in the back. Fear that got me stabbed in the back. It's fear. Just fear—always fear. Think about it, really think. We're all," he looked at Esar-Haden, "terrified."

"We should be," said Esar-Haden.

The man lowered his gaze to his hands. "I hated what I saw that night. I couldn't comprehend it. We killed the men then went back for their wives and children. On the way I asked my father why we did what we did. He said that, later, if we had taken the men prisoner, had allowed them to live, when they saw their wives and daughters breaking their backs in the mines or thrown to the military academy to be used as sex slaves, or worse yet, taken to Maljamir, given over to the demons, to entertain them with their suffering, when the fathers saw their sons taken into the bedrooms of the dark elf priestesses, where scars would collect on their once pristine skins, those men would rise up, start a slave rebellion."

"Humph," snorted Esar-Haden.

"He said it was better to kill them now," continued the dying man. "I remember thinking, if these men didn't fight now, if they laid down on their stomachs, knowing what was coming, if they—and then I thought, maybe it was that we had yanked them from their beds, they were shocked, they couldn't comprehend, they couldn't act because what was happening was so foreign, so overwhelming that it paralyzed them into inaction. But," he shook his head, "it just didn't make sense." He rest his head against the stone wall and closed his eyes. All the tension left his body. Thinking the man was dead, Esar-Haden began to creep toward him, intent on the daggers.

"I never wanted to see that again," said the man, his eyes opening. He pulled his head away from the wall. "I made myself incompetent at one thing and competent at another. I made myself into a lover. I'm handsome, charming. It wasn't hard to entice females. You know how they are. It wasn't hard to coil myself at their feet, even though I hated them, even though I hated myself for doing it. Still, I told myself, better that than to live and die by the sword. I thought I was doing myself a favor. Now I see it was nothing but fear." The man looked down, but not at the shafts of wood protruding from his chest, but past them, to some distant landscape in his mind. "What kind of life would I have led," he looked at Esar-Haden, "if I weren't afraid?"

"A short one," answered Esar-Haden. He continued, almost lecturing the man. "What are you now? A dying man—full of regret? Why blame yourself? Look at what we're born into. What are we supposed to do? We can't be blamed."

"An old soul," said the man. "Are you absolving me of my sins? Of my cowardice?" he asked. "A divine pardon delivered by a brothel whelp?"

"I'm house-born," Esar-Haden muttered under his breath.

The color blanched from the man's face. "Listen, boy, old soul or not, listen. I'm a dying man. I have something to say."

Esar-Haden looked to the alley's entrance. The sounds of battle were fading. The clean-up was almost over. 'If I don't claim those daggers,' Esar thought, glancing at the oh-so-close prize, 'I'll lose them to some other thieving bastard.' He advanced a bit further, glancing back at the brothel door, in case it had opened. It hadn't. He went to the man, crouched in front of him, his boots squelching in the man's blood. He reached between the man's legs and searched for the handles of the daggers. The man found enough strength to grab Esar-Haden's wrist.

"Don't waste your life, like I did. Try to imagine what you could do if you weren't afraid. If everyone is afraid, everyone around you, everyone you ever encounter, and you *aren't*." He squeezed Esar-Haden's wrist. "What kind of life would that be?"

"I don't know," whispered Esar-Haden. He looked down at the man's hand, then back up to his bloodied face.

"What's your name?" asked the man.

"Esar-Haden."

"Esar-Haden, those bulls, the ones with the demon's horns, they had empty eyes, as vacant as the desert dark. The men, their masters, had terror-filled eyes. Now, as I lay dying, my eyes see through theirs. I understand. You, Esar-Haden, you know what I couldn't comprehend on that horrible night. You know what dying men regret."

The man's grip weakened and his hand fell away. Esar-Haden pulled the twin daggers free. Beneath the blood that stained them glowed powerful enchantments.

He looked into the man's face. A noise, a door being unlatched, turned his gaze away. A flicker of light played on the stone hollow at the end of the alley. He saw the pale skin and fair hair of a surface girl as she peered around the corner. She held a candle in her trembling hand.

"Hold the door!" commanded Esar-Haden, beginning to rise. The man's grip returned, more sure than it had been before. He arrested Esar-Haden's momentum.

"Don't sell those daggers, boy," he commanded. "Use them, but not for some petty tyrant. Not for someone who is trying to use you, then discard you when they're done. Damn it, use them for yourself."

"I'm just a boy," whispered Esar-Haden.

"Not for long," countered the dying man.

"Then what?" Esar-Haden shook his head. "One man against the world?"

"One *fearless* man against the world."

Esar-Haden studied the dying man's eyes, watching them un-focus and struggle to focus again.

"That makes all the difference."

"Bring this man some wine," said Esar-Haden, turning to the prostitute. "Wine! Damn you!"

"He's dead," she protested.

Esar-Haden turned back to the man. A pair of empty eyes gazed back at him.

"Then I'll drink to him," he said, rising.

Beginning/End

A delicate perfume overrode the mingled aromas of food, wine, and gutter-stench clouding Ulat-Shen's street-side, open-air stall. It was not a scent Esar-Haden often encountered in the foul-smelling Ghetto of White Skin, a debauched neighborhood in the center of Pwyll, one of the many subterranean cities of the dark elf race.

"Esar-Haden?"

"Nope," he said, not looking up from his food.

"I'm sure of it."

"Got the wrong guy."

She slid onto the adjacent stool. He felt her hand on his thigh. "You fit his description."

He swallowed and looked at her. She was so gorgeous he was stunned. She wore a black cloak, hood up, head bent, but still looking at him. Her long white hair spilled out from the opening, framing her oval face. The front of her cloak was open and he saw she was dressed for a seduction.

"Looking for a lover?" he asked. "I can help, forget that other guy."

She smiled. "That's just what he would say."

"I thought you didn't know him." He turned and picked up a sushi. He wanted to eat them before Ulat-Shen passed by and they disappeared.

"I know everything about you, Esar-Haden. That's why I want to talk to you. I have a business—"

"Got more business than I can handle."

"I know all about that."

He looked at her. "Oh, that's right. You know everything about me."

The thought made him uncomfortable and he started to rise. She rose and slid her arm under his, tugging him into motion. Two men, both dark elves, stepped from the crowd and walked ahead of them, a second pair fell in behind.

Esar-Haden let her pull him along. He was thinking about the most recent spell Soléne had tried to teach him. He struggled to remember the words and how to pronounce them. He was still fumbling over the spell when the group arrived at the mouth of an alley. She pulled him in. The men remained at the entrance. Esar-Haden knew the alley. He knew there was only one way in or out.

"Doorman at Poquelin's Cabaret?" she asked, but it rang like an accusation. "More than a doorman, though. You practically run the place."

"I don't work too hard. Out of curiosity, what's your name? What house are you from?"

"You may call me Seka." She stood so her cloak was open. He couldn't help but admire her dual approach —the body and the muscle, the carrot and the stick. "It's not important what house I belong to, if I even do." She smirked. "From what my sources tell me you take a good percentage of the door."

"Shakedown?"

She chuckled and shook her head. "All that coin and you sleep in a hovel."

"I'm frugal."

"I like you," she said. "You're cute, capable, and creative, but you're undisciplined. You waste all your ill-gotten gains." She frowned. "Aren't much of a long-term thinker, are we?"

"You *really* do know me."

"What you need is a partner." She stepped up and wrapped her arms around his neck, brushing her lips against his. She breathed in his air and gave him hers.

"Someone to compensate for your shortcomings. I could do that for you."

"How charitable."

"But that's all in the future." She started to kiss him but pulled back.

"What about now?" he asked.

She gazed up into his eyes. "Now you're going to do me a favor."

. . .

Esar-Haden had to get out of the Ghetto of White Skin. It was all too much. He knew he was being followed. Seka had brought a fifth guy, a guy who knew what he was doing, who had been there the whole time, unseen.

Esar-Haden suspected as much. He figured she was the daughter of a powerful house, not some wannabe, like his own sisters. He knew the Skin. It didn't take long to spot her fifth man—then lose him.

Seka had put some effort into learning about him. He wanted her to understand that she didn't know everything. She had him sleeping in the hovel. That was true, but not every night.

. . .

"Esar!" exclaimed Soléne. "I swear, even though I built that magical portal, it surprises me every time." Soléne was standing in front of a full-length mirror, examining an outfit, a long, thin, black dress with a webbed back. It was little more than lingerie. A pile of rejected clothes was scattered on the bed.

Esar-Haden threw himself down on them.

"Esar! Those are expensive! Shoo! Shoo!" Soléne waved at him.

Esar stood up and walked to an overstuffed chair. He sat on the arm, watching Soléne.

She spun back to the mirror. "What are you doing here?" She looked over her shoulder. "Not that I'm not happy to see you."

"Had to ditch a tail."

Soléne looked at Esar-Haden's reflection in the mirror.

"Nothing to worry about."

"Do I need to turn somebody to stone?" enquired Soléne, still looking at Esar-Haden through the mirror.

"All depends. I might be getting in over my head." He looked into the mirror, into Soléne's large, dark eyes. "You may have to rescue me."

"I *may* have to lock you up and never let you out."

"But then how would I get into trouble?"

"What is it this time? Robbery, smuggling?" She paused, speaking again in a conspiratorial tone. "Assassination?"

"Seating."

"Huh?"

"Seating the right people at the right table. Keeping the wrong people out in the street."

Soléne tossed the outfit, rushed over to Esar-Haden, and leapt into his lap. She wrapped one thin arm around his neck, took up a few strands of her long hair, and began to twirl them. "Tell me everything. You know I love gossip."

. . .

"I'm going with you."

"What?"

"I'm going with you to work tonight," said Soléne, getting up out of his lap.

Esar-Haden sat up. "You hate the Skin."

"I have to find the right outfit," mumbled Soléne.

Esar-Haden frowned.

. . .

"I hate when you sulk," said Soléne.

The pair walked towards the Ghetto of White Skin.

"I don't see—"

"I'm a known entity," interrupted Soléne. "People will recognize me."

"But no makeup, those clothes, and you're carrying yourself like—"

"A man?" Soléne chuckled. "Quit being such a baby. We're two males going to the Skin. Nothing unusual about that." Soléne reached out and touched Esar-Haden's cheek. "Let me play in your world for one night."

. . .

"A bit chilling, isn't it?" enquired Erodu, turning away from his simulacrum, a magically created copy of himself. It was without consciousness, otherwise it was an exact, living replica. It lay on a table, covered with a sheet to hide its nudity.

"How does it work?" asked Zai, the matron mother of House Grixx.

"It's quite simple," began Erodu. He turned, looking for somewhere to sit but found nothing. The room was cramped, having just enough space for the table. He turned back to the simulacrum. "Should I become injured, the wounds are transferred to the—" He motioned with his hand to the body breathing under the sheet.

"You remain uninjured?"

"Yes." Erodu smiled. "Amazing what you can do with magic." Erodu smoothed out a wrinkle in his elaborate robe. "There *is* one thing," he looked at Zai. "It doesn't last. The magic unravels, the body decomposes."

"How long?"

"A few days at most. Long enough for what you need, if you act fast. It's a difficult spell. The components are rare and the cost exorbitant. When I came across the

65

spell I was dismayed. It seemed exceedingly useful and nearly impossible to afford, in practical terms." He smiled. "Then inspiration struck. You see, I create two. Double the expense, but the usefulness pays for it, and allows for a profit. I leave that with you." He nodded towards the simulacrum. "I'll leave one with House Ah-Trayik. Should one side ambush the other I will no doubt be caught in the fray. The wounds will show up on both copies. Of course, the aggressor won't be surprised. The betrayed house; however, will know at once that their trust has been misplaced." He unconsciously ran a hand over his long beard. "Not to mention, should I personally be insulted with a betrayal of my trust," he looked up into her beautiful, cruel face. "I will exhaust every avenue available to annihilate my newfound enemy."

Matron Mother Zai Grixx smiled, but it was not friendly. "Have you met Matron Mother Rovina Ah-Trayik?"

"I haven't had the pleasure."

"So they don't yet have a simulacrum of you?"

He shook his head.

In a flash of movement Zai reached behind her, slid a dagger out of its sheath, and thrust it into the surprised wizard's neck. She yanked towards her, pulling the blade through the wizard's wind pipe. Where there should have been a fatal wound there was only age-spotted flesh. Zai spun and looked down at the simulacrum.

It convulsed on the table. Gurgling sounds came from the wound as the blood filled its severed airway. Erodu watched in shock as the blood soaked into the once pristine sheet. The body sounded a final sickening gurgle, then lie still.

Zai Grixx reached out and grabbed the wizard's beard, turning his face to hers. "Had to be sure. Lucky for you it works." She glanced to the body, then back to

Erodu. "I hope you brought enough of those rare and expensive spell components."

She released his beard and smoothed it. She stepped past him, opened the door, and stepped into the hall. One of her daughters, standing at attention outside of the door, turned to face her. "When our esteemed guest is finished with his fancy spell," said Zai, "show him out, then come back and keep an eye on that thing in there—the," she made air quotes, "living one."

"Yes, Matron Mother."

. . .

Poquelin's Cabaret was full of rowdy men. It was one of the only places in all of Pwyll in which a dark elf male, no matter his station, could be treated well. In Poquelin's he could be the master of his domain—until his coin purse had been emptied.

There were plenty of women in the large room; women of all types and races from the surface. They sat in laps, flirted, kissed, teased, and whispered their knowledge and enthusiasm for the carnal pleasures into pointed, ebony ears. Their talents were in feeding the male ego.

Women with still more talent could be found on stage, singing, dancing, performing ribald skits, and reciting the poetry of love and lust. Many of these women were also skilled in the art of lovemaking and could be had —for a price.

Esar-Haden's keen eyes saw every interaction. He made it his business to intervene in every romance, to ensure the right amount of coin was exchanged, and that the secretive owners of Poquelin's Cabaret got their cut.

He shut the front door and looked up into the face of a gnoll, a seven foot tall half-human, half-hyena named Kiula. "No one else but regulars, understand?" Kiula curled back her lips, revealing black and pink spotted gums and gleaming white fangs. "I don't care how much coin they stuff in your paw, or how many threats they utter. I'm serious. If you don't recognize them, tell them to —" He smiled and winked.

He reached into his jacket and produced a large emerald. He let it flash in the light from the chandeliers. Kiula glanced down at it. She looked back to Esar-Haden. She reached down and ran the tip of her thumb over the exposed blade of her battle axe. Esar-Haden tossed the gem. Kiula deftly plucked it from the air. "If you think you need more of a bribe than that, you're worse than a dark elf," muttered Esar-Haden, turning away from the gnoll.

He glanced at a table at the rear. A lone "male" sat, hidden in an oversized cloak. A pair of glasses and a bottle of red wine sat on the table. He looked to a large semi-circular table at the front of the stage. Two males sat on one side, two on the other side. In between them sat a male from the surface—a wizard in elaborate robes.

Clinging to his arm was a surface woman, one the wizard had brought with him. She was dressed as elaborately and as richly as he was. She wore a pale yellow dress, her blonde hair held in place with diamond-studded pins, and was clearly highborn. Her skin and teeth were too perfect to be anything less than noble in birth.

Esar-Haden suspected the wizard had offered to take her on a trip to the fabled and dangerous city of the dark elves. She would, he no doubt promised, be absolutely safe, so long as she stayed by his side.

She was also pregnant. It wasn't obvious. She wasn't too far along and the dress hid her growing middle. But Esar-Haden had pulled her chair for her. He noticed how she reached for her stomach when she sat. He wondered if it was the wizard's. Bringing his pregnant bride to Pwyll was an idiotic idea.

He knew that no matter how powerful one was, there was always someone or something more dangerous out there. He also knew, from long experience, that when one got involved in house politics one had to take every precaution. The wizard, it seemed, was too arrogant to bother.

Esar-Haden looked to Orm, the black-bearded dwarf behind the bar, and nodded. Orm nodded back, stepped over to a rope-pull, and yanked twice. Esar-Haden knew a bell was ringing back stage. He made his way through the crowd until he reached the small, high table at the back. He sat and glanced at Soléne.

"How long do we have to wait?" she whispered.

"Not long," grumbled Esar-Haden.

"Oh, cheer up," chastised Soléne. "Aren't we having fun?"

Esar-Haden scowled.

"Is that your 'I'm serious' work face?" she asked, reaching under the table to pinch his inner thigh.

"I hate you," he mumbled.

"Such a drama queen," joked Soléne. "That's them, isn't it? No house markings."

"I went to the military academy with one of them."

"What house is he from?"

"Hell if I remember," admitted Esar-Haden.

A dark elf male parted the black velvet curtains and stepped out. His costume was that of a surface wizard; black robes with arcane symbols stitched in silver thread, his shoulders covered with raven feathers, a long, twisted wooden staff held in one hand. When he saw an actual surface wizard sitting at his feet, he bowed. He rose and began his spiel.

Esar had heard it many times. He bent and was about to whisper in Soléne's ear when he noticed a pair of eyes that were not on the presenter, but on him. The male

69

sat by himself, near the corner of the room, scowling at Esar-Haden. It took him a moment to recognize the fifth of Seka's men, the professional among them.

'How did he get in here,' he asked himself.

"—necromancer or transmutationist."

"Huh?"

"Haven't you been listening?" asked Soléne.

"No."

"I think he's a necromancer or a transmutationist."

"You can tell that just by looking?"

"His robes, silly. He has symbols from those two schools stitched into his robes. Protection spells, I imagine. Rather obvious, but perhaps that's the point."

"Should I be worried?"

"Are you going to attack him?"

"Hadn't planned on it."

"Then don't worry." Soléne took a drink of wine. "They aren't well known symbols. He's no novice." She looked to Esar-Haden. "You remember yet what house he's from?" She nodded to the male dark elf Esar-Haden had recognized.

"I didn't know I was supposed to be remembering that."

"Esar-Haden, if I have to piece all of this together for you I'm going to want a cut of your gold."

"Speaking of—" said Esar. He saw a man reaching into his coin purse. The woman in his lap was smiling and holding out her hand. He rose from the table and made his way over to the eager couple.

· · ·

"You follow those two," whispered Soléne. "I'll follow those two."

Esar-Haden, Soléne, and the gnoll stood at the front door.

"Haven't you had enough fun?" asked Esar.

"You need my help."

"You're going to get yourself hurt," he warned. "It's two on one and you don't even have a weapon."

"Oh, silly boy."

"What about the wizard?" asked Esar-Haden. "Who'll follow him?"

"No need. He'll stay in the Skin. The nicest place he can find. Hurry, Esar, they're getting away." Soléne darted through the door and fell in behind the pair of dark elves.

"Lock up, will ya?" he called out to Orm. "I guess my night's just getting started." The dwarf nodded. Esar-Haden exited the cabaret.

He began to follow the other pair of males. The duo made a few other stops in the Ghetto of White Skin. They darted through a alleys and meandered their way from neighborhood to neighborhood. 'Working awfully hard to lose any tails,' thought Esar-Haden, as he once again dodged out of sight. 'I guarantee the others have shaken Soléne by now.'

· · ·

Soléne had learned what she wanted to learn, and was taking a round-about way back home. She was feeling rather self-congratulatory when an arm shot from the darkness, a hand wrapped around her throat. It was Seka's fifth man. A dagger flashed and was held with the point just below her jaw.

"Who are you?" he whispered.

Soléne closed her eyes and concentrated. The male wasn't choking her, merely holding her. He was standing behind her, hiding himself. This meant he couldn't see her lips. Soléne began to whisper the words of a spell. She traced unnatural shapes with her fingers. The man didn't notice.

"A buddy of Esar-Haden's?" he asked. "Whatever angle you two are working it ain't worth it. This thing's bigger than either of you. I promise, you ain't getting paid enough. Tell me what you know and we can work this out."

Soléne's voice rose above a whisper as the final words of the spell passed her lips.

"What's that?" asked her assailant.

"Just a little spell."

"What?" asked the male, digging the tip of his dagger into Soléne's flesh. The cut was slight, but Soléne relished the note of pain. She felt the line of blood run down her neck.

The man watched with surprise as the long, white hair of his captive began to float. He tried to press the dagger in deeper, to squeeze Soléne's neck tighter, but the hair snaked around his wrists and took control of his actions. The magicked hair pulled his arms out wide. He struggled to break free but couldn't. He tried to yell but hair wrapped around his throat and constricted, silencing him.

Soléne turned to face her attacker. She was surrounded by a crown of "living" hair. Some coiled like a serpent ready to strike. The rest bound the man. Soléne looked to the dagger. With a mental command her hair shook the man's wrist. The dagger clattered to the ground.

Soléne's hair wrapped around the man's face, covering his nose and mouth, leaving an opening for his eyes. Still more hair snaked around his throat. With a thought the magicked hair constricted. The man began to convulse as his lungs struggled to draw air. Soléne watched as panic and fear flashed in the man's eyes. The pair stood in silence as his life was pulled from him by the "living" hair.

Soléne commanded her hair to release her attacker. His corpse crumpled at her feet. She knelt and looked into his lifeless eyes. "*Now* I've had enough fun." She rose, turned, and made her way home.

. . .

"House Ah-Trayik," concluded Soléne.

"The other?"

"Not sure, yet," admitted Soléne. "Whichever house it is, they're being careful."

"What's up with the dried blood on your neck?"

"Hold me, Esar."

"I *am* holding you."

"Hold me tighter."

. . .

Esar-Haden sat on a stone bench that was umbrellaed by a giant gold-green mushroom. He hated that they, House Koi Ki, who "controlled" the Ghetto of White Skin, let these enormous, stupid looking mushrooms grow in the filth and rotting refuse that was swept into the gutters by the street merchants. Every time he saw one he wanted to cut it down but he had heard that Matron Mother Taschen herself liked them, saying they added charm to an otherwise ugly section of town.

The dark elf rogue glanced from the fleshy gills above him to a pair of fleshy, bare legs belonging to one of the surface females brought into the caves of Pwyll to entertain, by choice or force, the restless dark elves. She passed out of view. He returned his attention to the food stall across the street. A pair of large eyes set atop a frog-like head could be seen glancing over the heads of those sitting at the counter.

A customer pushed his bowl and cup away from him then reached into his jacket for his money pouch. He tossed a few copper coins onto the counter. Ulat-Shen reached over the heads of his seated customers and

73

extended his long, webbed fingers, careful not to let his forearm fin hit anyone. He waved Esar-Haden over.

"Sweet beans and sushi—two."

"Two!" cried Ulat-Shen. "Do you know how hard it is to get fish through the desert above, down here into these miserable caves, and keep it fresh? It cost a fortune! You want two?"

"How about three?" asked Esar-Haden. "Two for me and one for you." He reached into a pocket and tossed a pair of gold coins onto the counter. "And don't lie. I know you get your fish from an underground lake."

"You know a lot. You big-time-operator now, huh?" asked Ulat-Shen. He swept the coins off of the counter, into his apron pocket. He spun and began to prepare Esar-Haden's sushi.

"And wine," added Esar-Haden.

Ulat-Shen's assistant, a goblin, small, green-skinned, and stupid, stepped up onto the box behind the counter and placed a ceramic cup in front of the dark elf. Even with the assistance of the box the goblin was barely tall enough to reach the counter. Esar-Haden could only make out the goblin's large, dull eyes, and his long, pointed nose, which drug along the counter, leaving a trail of snot.

The goblin giggled as he poured the steaming wine into the cup and waited. Esar-Haden eyed him. He didn't like the giggle. He downed the contents in one gulp and set the cup back. The goblin refilled it, spilling wine on his own nose, and giggled at whatever mystery he alone knew then descended out of sight.

Ulat-Shen turned and set a small plate and a shallow bowl in front of Esar-Haden. The bowl held a pile of heavily seasoned, bright-green beans. The plate held three rectangles of tofu with a sliver of orange fish atop them all wrapped in what appeared to be dark-green seaweed. Before Esar-Haden could make a move, Ulat-Shen produced a pair of chopsticks and plucked one of the sushi from the plate. He deftly popped it into his mouth. He half bowed to Esar-Haden, his head fin waving. When he stood back up his eyes settled on something or someone behind his customer.

Esar-Haden glanced over his shoulder.

"I'm mad at you," said Seka.

"I thought things went well."

"Eat fast."

. . .

Seka led Esar-Haden by the arm. This time they didn't go to the alley, but to his one-room hovel. He noticed she wasn't dressed for a seduction, but for the possibility of combat. He guessed the honeymoon was over. As they approached the door a dark elf male stepped out.

"It's safe," he said to Seka. He sneered at Esar-Haden.

She led him through the doorway. Esar-Haden noted the lock had been busted. She pushed him into the small room and shut the door. He turned to face her. She advanced and pushed him backwards onto the bed. He fell onto his butt, his back against the wall.

She lifted her leg and placed one stiletto-heeled boot between his legs. Esar-Haden looked up at her and tried to discern her mood. She helped him by smiling. "My faith in you was well placed," she said, bending forward to rest her elbow on her knee, chin on her fist. "The first meeting went just as I'd hoped."

"And that made you mad?"

"I know."

"Know what?"

"You ditched him once, was it too much trouble to ditch him twice? Good help is hard to find." The blank look in Esar-Haden's face made her curious. "You have no idea what I'm talking about, do you?" Esar-Haden shook his head. "You didn't kill him?"

Esar-Haden pieced everything together. Seka's man must have followed Soléne. He wondered if Soléne had killed him, she hadn't mentioned it. Then again, she was in an unusual mood last night, and there was the cut on her neck.

"I didn't kill your guy."

"Well," said Seka. "That worries me. Now I have to find out who *did* kill him and why?"

"It's a dangerous city."

She chuckled at his observation. "I want you to secure a private place for a second meeting," she said. "Private, understand? Make sure it can seat four people."

"A few places come to mind."

"Don't tell anyone." She lifted her foot from the bed and stood. She produced a pouch from the folds of her cloak and tossed it on the mattress. He heard the jingle of coin. "Privacy is everything. I'm going to be attending this meeting myself."

. . .

"You can't be serious," complained Seka. "Your hovel?" She looked at him. "There isn't even enough room."

"I cleared everything out and borrowed four chairs." Seka began to protest. Esar-Haden cut her off. "Look." He nodded to one end of the narrow alley. Seka frowned at being silenced, but looked. It took her a moment to pick out the crouching form of a gnoll, partially hidden by a massive stalagmite. "There," Esar nodded to the other end of the alley. Seka followed his eyes to Orm, standing in the middle of the alleyway's entrance, propping himself up on a war hammer that was nearly as tall as he was. "All cordoned off. No front doors open into this alley. I may live in the ghetto, but I live smart."

Seka nodded to one of her men. He left the alley. She looked at Esar-Haden, shook her head, and stepped into his back-alley shack. Esar-Haden followed. Before too long the door opened and an unknown male stepped into the room. He looked at both Esar-Haden and Seka. He leaned out of the doorway and spoke to someone outside. He stepped back into the room and sat in the empty chair across from Esar-Haden. A female dark elf stepped into the room. She eyed Esar-Haden and Seka with obvious distain. One of Seka's men shut the door.

'Soléne was right,' mused Esar-Haden, 'Anna Ah-Trayik.' He averted his gaze, as was expected of a male.

"What's this!" hissed the eldest daughter of House Ah-Trayik. "Where is Zai Grixx?"

'Grixx!' Thought Esar-Haden. He looked sidelong at Seka. Perspiration beaded on her forehead at the mention of the name. She looked at him. Their eyes met. He read her thoughts. 'She screwed up inviting me to this.' He controlled his demeanor, looking nonplused. He even went so far as to examine the dirt beneath his fingernails.

Anna Ah-Trayik turned towards the door.

"My matron mother," Seka stood as she spoke, "is cautious, but serious."

'I certainly am learning a lot,' thought Esar-Haden.

Anna turned and looked at Seka. The hovel was so tight the two women stood breasts-to-breasts. The mood in the room was tense.

Esar-Haden looked to the other male. He had his hand on the hilt of his sword, looking at Seka. Esar-Haden smiled. He knew the room was too tight for the man to draw and effectively use a blade that long. Esar-Haden slid out one of his daggers and held it at the side of his thigh.

"I am Seka Grixx. I speak for my matron mother, with her permission." She sat down.

Anna glared at Seka. "Never heard of you. I know all the daughters of House Grixx."

Seka looked sidelong at Esar-Haden yet again. She looked to Anna. "I'm an Alamuti Ascetic. I was taken to their monastery at birth."

'Well damn,' thought Esar-Haden.

"Grixx has an ascetic?" Anna studied Seka. The revelation had reduced her arrogance by half. "Your house is full of surprises." She sat. She leaned her head to her male bodyguard. "I should have brought fifty males." She smiled. "That is if she really is an ascetic, or even a daughter of House Grixx."

"If this was a trap, you'd be dead already," observed Esar-Haden. He sheathed his dagger with a sigh of defeated resignation.

Anna turned sharply to him. "How dare you address me!"

Esar-Haden looked at her. He was in no mood for proper etiquette. He wasn't even sure he was going to leave the meeting alive. 'I know too much now because of your big mouth,' he thought. 'If only you'd had some tact.' He condemned her, silently. Still, despite his change of mood, he regretted his outburst.

"Despite the male's," Seka looked from Anna to Esar, then back to Anna, "insolence, may I remind you, we have much more important matters to discuss."

"About time," muttered Anna, looking away from Esar-Haden.

"Our houses have been warring for a generation," continued Seka. "We've wasted our energies tearing each other down for too long. Meanwhile our common foe," she glanced at Esar-Haden, "grows more powerful." She looked back at her hoped-for ally. "If our houses continue along this path for another generation we'll leave nothing for our mutual enemy to destroy." Anna nodded in agreement. Seka continued. "Matron Mother Grixx feels that our houses should combine forces."

A sinister smile spread across Anna's face. "The enemy of my enemy is my friend."

"We have been at war for so long few would suspect us of uniting against a third."

"Zai certainly is clever," stated Anna.

"She's smart. This is the smart thing to do."

"She's paranoid," argued Anna. "More than most dark elves." She eyed Seka. "An ascetic *and* a surface wizard. She's taking every precaution."

"Matron Mother Zai wants the final meeting to go well. There's a great deal at stake."

"Zai fears an attempt on her life?" Anna chuckled. "House Ah-Trayik fears nothing and no one," she boasted. "We may be smaller than Grixx but we've fought you to a standstill for years."

Seka ignored the jab. "That must come to an end."

Anna smiled. "After a generation of war a daughter of House Ah-Trayik and a daughter of House Grixx have met without bloodshed." She laughed. "All according to Zai's plan. Set the third meeting. I hope Zai recognizes the patience Matron Mother Rovina shows by allowing her to control things at this early stage. It won't be that way for long." Anna looked around the hovel, smirking. She stood, as did her bodyguard.

"The matron mother of House Grixx sends her regards to your matron mother," said Seka, also rising. Esar-Haden rose. Seka and the male had their backs to him. Anna was facing Seka, ignoring the male who had dared violate her authority. Anna looked into the face of her rival, for they were still rivals until the matron mothers of both houses met.

"Together we will destroy House Isuph," said Anna Ah-Trayik.

Esar-Haden was glad no one saw the look of shock on his face. 'House Isuph!' he thought. 'Soléne!'

Anna Ah-Trayik and her bodyguard left the hovel. Seka stood in the doorway watching them pass out of the alley. She slammed the door and spun on Esar-Haden. "What was that!" she screamed. She grabbed his jacket and pushed him backwards until he slammed into the wall. The flimsy boards shook. "You couldn't keep your mouth shut for five minutes?"

"It was her," Esar-Haden nodded towards the chair in which Anna Ah-Trayik had sat, "who couldn't keep *her* mouth shut."

"If she had demanded your death I would have given it to her."

"And here I thought we were starting to trust one another."

Seka yanked him from the wall and slammed him back into it. She released him and plopped down into a chair. She bent forward and placed her elbows on her knees. "It's my fault," she admitted. She glanced at Esar-Haden. "You should have been outside, with the others." She sat up. "Truth is, I was scared. I didn't want to be in here alone with them. They could have killed me. Zai is taking a huge risk. House Ah-Trayik could use this as an opportunity to betray us and turn the tide of battle their way." She looked at Esar-Haden, who had not even bothered to straighten his jacket. "Surprised at my honesty?"

"Surprised at your worry. I thought Alamuti Ascetics were fearless." He pushed himself from the wall and pulled down the hem of his jacket.

Seka scoffed. "You believed that lie?" She shook her head. "An ascetic would never rely on a rogue male." She laughed. "They wouldn't need to." She looked at him. "You should know that."

Esar-Haden sat down across from her. He was about to speak but Seka anticipated his question.

"I'm not a daughter of House Grixx. I'm a hired hand, just like you. Expendable, just like you." She smiled at Esar-Haden. "You're really in a fix now." She reached out and patted his knee. "Don't worry. I'm not going to kill you."

"Thanks."

"I can't let you out of my sight until this is all over."

"Until the third meeting is over or until House Isuph is over?" He thought of Soléne. House Isuph had been dominant for so long that it was difficult to imagine it any other way. 'You've certainly led a charmed life,' Esar thought of his lover. 'If your house had been at war all these years you would have not been allowed to satisfy your lust with a low-born male.' The line of thought was depressing.

He looked at Seka. She seemed to be pondering the answer to his question. He wondered, though, if he cared enough to risk his life for Soléne. He had always gone his own way, a loner, looking out for himself. 'Would she risk her life for me,' he asked himself. 'A gutter rat? A lover she sneaks in and out of her chambers?' He was careful not to frown. 'Does she care, or am I merely entertaining her?' That line of thought was as depressing as the first. He gave it up for the time being. 'House Grixx.' He looked away from Seka. He glanced to the empty chair next to him, picturing its most recent occupant, 'House Ah-Trayik.' He worked hard to hide his consternation and worry from the female across from him. 'Damn it, Esar, what are you going to do?'

"I thought this was easy money," he muttered.

"No such thing," muttered Seka.

. . .

Now wearing a dress of light blue with touches of gold thread, Princess Daphnia roamed the open bazaar. She eyed the bodyguard hired by Erodu. "You annoy me," she stated. He looked at her but did not reply. "You stand too close and you're hideous." She turned over an expertly crafted hair pin. It was silver with gold inlay. She was reminded of one of the suitors her father had tempted her with. "Tall and thin, he looks like a pin!" She repeated the insult she had turned the suitor away with and tossed the pin back into the wooden case from which she had plucked it. She turned to the male dark elf. "Can't you stand up straight?"

"An old wound, Mistress."

"You're bent like a piece of greenwood, dried behind the stove." She laughed. "That's what I'll call you, Greenwood the Ugly." She smirked, enjoying her own humor. She glanced from him to the crowded street. She decided Pwyll, for all its exotic charm, was beneath her. She regretted coming. Still, she hated to be away from Erodu, now that she carried his son. She was certain it was a son. 'My father tried every suitor,' she thought. 'I chose my own.' She looked back to the male. 'Look how weak and pathetic he is. Not like my Erodu. He could bring this whole city down.'

"Manners, manners. Remember you're a guest here."

Princess Daphnia turned to the speaker. A female dark elf stood too close. Daphnia looked to her bodyguard, he was gone. Two males she didn't recognize stood in his place. She looked back to the female dark elf.

"I'm Princess—"

"I know who you are," interrupted the female from House Grixx.

"Leave me alone," warned Daphnia, her voice wavering. "My husband is Erodu the Great, High Wizard of—"

The female dark elf slid a dagger from the sheath at her belt, silencing the princess. The blade glinted in the magical floating globes illuminating the bazaar. Daphnia looked at it, stunned. "I can't be touched," she whispered. "He said I can't be touched."

The female from House Grixx reached out and took the surface woman's arm. She pulled her into motion. The tip of her dagger found its way to Daphnia's side, passed through the blue and gold fabric, and bit into her skin, but not deep enough to hurt her.

"Is it true you're pregnant?" she asked, her voice smoother than the surface of the discarded hair pin.

. . .

"You're brilliant, sadistic, but brilliant," whispered Seka as she bent next to Esar-Haden, undressing, as was he. "Look how pissed off everyone is."

Esar-Haden looked around the cave. It was longer than it was wide with only one way in. The cave was filled with steaming water, a hot spring. Only a narrow edge of stone allowed one to skirt the pool. The spring itself was shaped like the number eight. 'For once my time at the military academy paid off,' he thought.

The hot spring, a healthy distance from the main caves of Pwyll, was a favorite hideout for the cadets of the military academy. They could sneak away from their instructors, absconding with a couple of bottles of wine, and relax in the hot water, releasing the stress in their bruised and battered bodies.

He knew that the matron mothers of House Ah-Trayik and House Grixx would be unfamiliar with the hot spring, which made it an ideal location. Neither house wanted the other to have an advantage. He glanced at Seka. 'Not even she'd heard of it.'

Seka had been reluctant to leave the city in order to scout the site, despite his reassurances. Since the second meeting she had been on edge and paranoid. She knew her mistake, inviting him to the second meeting resulted in a threat to his life. She suspected he wanted to escape her control. She was right, but not entirely for the right reasons.

As they had scoured the city, Esar-Haden looked for any opportunity to ditch Seka and her henchmen, all to no avail. He needed to warn Soléne, while something could be done, when the alliance against her house could actually be stopped. Seka's extreme paranoia and watchful eye, not to mention the constant presence of her henchmen, had made escape impossible.

He glanced at Seka's pile of clothing. She had sent her henchmen back to Pwyll, ostensibly to make all parties concerned more comfortable. Esar-Haden frowned. Now was his opportunity to escape, but it was too late. He doubted he could make it all the way to Soléne to warn her. It didn't matter. He had already accepted his fate.

He noticed that Anna Ah-Trayik was staring at him, her face twisted in anger. She was reluctantly undressing. The very idea of holding the secret meeting at a hot spring, all parties required to skinny dip, was incredibly insulting. It was also desirable. With all parties vulnerable, the power dynamic had been equalized. Anna caught the attention of her matron mother.

Rovina Ah-Trayik stood in perfect nudity. Her hair was held up by some elaborate, glittering piece of jewelry. Other than that she was bare. A male stood next to her, also naked, holding mother and daughter's clothing and weapons, as well as his own. At her daughter's direction Matron Mother Rovina looked to Esar-Haden. Her bearing was regal, commanding, and intimidating, despite her nudity. She smiled at Esar-Haden and nodded. She found his selection amusing.

"Where's Zai?" growled Anna Ah-Trayik.

Seka walked to the cave's entrance. "I directed them to take the longer route here." She looked from the tunnel to Anna. "I thought it would be poor form to have you all bump into each other in the tunnels leading here."

Matron Mother Rovina chuckled but didn't acknowledge the speaker. She eased herself into the pool. Anna followed. Their male attendants began to carefully arrange the group's combined weapons and clothing on the slippery ledge of stone.

It had been decided that the males, Esar-Haden included, were to occupy the pool nearest the cave's entrance. The surface wizard was excluded from this. He was going to sit between the matron mothers, fulfilling his duties as negotiator and safeguard against betrayal.

The wizard had protested the loudest to the hot spring. Esar-Haden knew why. The protective spells stitched into his robes meant little if he wasn't wearing them. The wizard, still complaining, lowered his aged, naked body into the water. Finding the temperature agreeable he submersed himself to the chin, his beard floating, and began to maneuver between the pools. His mood changed. He reminded himself that he was invulnerable for the time being thanks to his twin simulacrums. He rolled onto his back and floated.

. . .

Matron Mother Zai Grixx stood alone in the cramped room, having sent her daughter out in the hall to wait for her command. Elsewhere in House Grixx her males were armed and ready for battle. Zai Grixx stared down at the wizard's simulacrum. She reached out, grabbed the edge of the blanket, and threw it from the

85

body. She ran her hand just above the breathing but silent mass, feeling its warmth. She wanted to smile, but would wait.

. . .

Esar-Haden glanced around the cave. Seka was still at the entrance, peering down the tunnel that led back to Pwyll. Daughter and mother were conversing. The males were wading into the water. The wizard floated on his back, studying the contours of the cave's ceiling and the twin magical orbs that lit the small space. For the moment no eyes were on Esar-Haden. He knew it was time but hesitated. He was hung up on how this all ended—with him dead. It made him a little sad.

'Despite all your grumbling,' he told himself, 'you actually enjoy life.' He frowned. 'Will she even know?' He wondered if and how Soléne would learn of his final heroic act. 'I would have never guessed—a martyr to love.' He realized he was staring at the wizard's water-speckled beard. He shook his head clear and took a deep breath. He made one last sweep of the room with his eyes then knelt and grabbed the handles of his daggers.

He glanced at Seka. She turned and was watching him. The look on her face was not what he expected, but he didn't have time to think about it. He stood, flipped the daggers in the air and caught them by the tips. He launched himself into the air and lifted his legs, compacting his body into a tight ball.

His activity drew the attention of everyone in the pool. He lifted his arms above his head. The two males began to turn in the water, thinking about their weapons. Anna Ah-Trayik began to move as well, trying to get between the airborne male, his daggers, and her mother. The wizard, seeing something quite unexpected in the air above him, started to right himself. Rovina Ah-Trayik did not lose, not even for an instant, her regal bearing. Her dark eyes watched Esar-Haden as if his actions had nothing to do with her.

Esar brought his arms down, throwing first one dagger, then the other. The gleaming streaks of silver crossed the space. Their reflections danced on the surface of the spring. The first dagger hit Anna Ah-Trayik in the chest. The second dagger, having glided along a separate but similar path, struck Rovina Ah-Trayik in the divot at the base of her throat.

Esar-Haden thrust his legs down with all the strength he could muster. One of his heels struck the wizard on the bridge of his nose, the other on his corner of his cheek bone. Having overshot the wizard, Esar dropped into the pool just in front of him. He reached up and behind him, attempting to grab the wizard. His fingers grasped at air. His head went beneath the water.

He kept himself submerged, swimming forward, eyes open. He wanted to get away from the wizard, or get to his daggers, he wasn't sure. He wasn't thinking, but operating on battle instinct. As he swam, Rovina Ah-Trayik sunk beneath the surface. Her face was as perfectly composed as a statue's, and equally as lifeless. A pair of arms reached into the water, grabbing for her. She slipped through them.

A pair of arms reached for Esar-Haden and caught him. He was pulled to the surface. One of the males had him. Esar lifted his feet, placed them against the male's chest, and thrust. The two flew apart. Esar went back under the water.

He came back up in the center of the pool. Anna Ah-Trayik was behind him, clutching her chest, glassy-eyed, paused in the act of climbing onto the thin ledge of stone. Her breathing was loud, ragged. A vivid line of blood ran down from the dagger between her breasts. Esar spun, anticipating threats from the other direction. What he saw surprised him. Seka was airborne. The males had turned their attention from him to the new arrival. The wizard was attempting to concentrate on a spell.

Judging from Seka's arc she was intent on interrupting the wizard. This threw Esar off. He paused, unsure. He had expected Seka to come for him, along with the males, and the wizard. Seka turned her head to the side. Her shoulder struck the wizard in the back of his neck. Her momentum carried both of them under the water. The water of the spring was turning red.

. . .

The wizard's simulacrum jerked. Water began to spill from its parted lips and flow from its nostrils. Zai Grixx smiled. She placed her hand on the grey-haired chest. The body convulsed beneath her touch. "He's drowning."

Her curiosity begged to know what exactly was happening at the third and final meeting. She hoped Seka would survive to tell her. She turned from the dying simulacrum, walked to the door, and opened it. Her daughter turned to face her.

"Begin the attack," commanded Zai. She glanced back at the simulacrum, watched its final tortured convulsions, then shut the door.

. . .

"Tell me again, Esar," begged Soléne. She wrapped her arms around her lover.

"I'm sleepy."

"I know, I just want to hear it again." Soléne lifted her face to Esar-Haden's and kissed him. She pulled back and looked into his eyes. "My savior. I'm surprised."

"You already said that."

"I am, though." Soléne studied her lover's face. "I never thought you would risk your life for me. It's *too* romantic."

"I didn't know I would either."

Soléne propped herself up on her elbow. "Seka certainly fooled you. She really did know everything about you, about *us*." Soléne pursed her lips. "I guess we aren't as much of a secret as I thought. Zai Grixx knows. I wonder who else? She certainly didn't waste the knowledge."

"She took a hell of a gamble."

"You think?" asked Soléne.

"How did she know I would do it, go after Rovina?"

"Well," Soléne thought. "Either you would or you wouldn't. If you did, you would either succeed," she smiled at her lover, "or fail. If you succeeded, she gets what she wanted, Rovina Ah-Trayik dead. If you failed, so what? She would reveal our secret and blame my house. Claiming Seka had been betrayed by you; which, technically she was. Sure, Ah-Trayik would be angry, the truce would be off, but Zai wouldn't be making a new enemy, just keeping an old one. I don't see a downside for her. It's quite a brilliant plan. I'm impressed. If only I could get to know Zai better. I could learn from her."

"Better not."

"Oh?"

"She's going to turn that strategic mind to your house next. Are you worried?"

"Nah, it will take her years to rebuild her strength. She has to keep a low profile for a bit. Despite the success of her little plot, House Ah-Trayik went down fighting. I heard she suffered significant losses assaulting their compound."

"Maybe she's vulnerable. Your house going to attack?"

Soléne shrugged a shoulder. "Not for me to decide."

"Ah, well, I'll rest easy for a night, then. I've earned it," said Esar-Haden. He lifted his arms and placed his hands behind his head.

"So Seka didn't kill you, huh?" asked Soléne.

"She let me walk away."

"She didn't want to tie up loose ends?"

"We have an understanding," said Esar, winking.

"Birds of a feather?"

"Something like that."

"Remind me about the wizard," said Soléne. "He didn't drown?"

"Somehow not," said Esar-Haden. "Seka held him under long enough that he should have."

"Maybe a water breathing spell," said Soléne. "Or something else. Transmutation is an amazing school of magic. So why didn't he kill all of you?"

"The princess."

Soléne looked at Esar.

"Zai was holding her hostage. Seka informed him —when he came up for air."

"He gave a damn about *her*?" asked Soléne.

"She's pregnant with his child," said Esar-Haden. "Didn't you notice?"

"No." Soléne rest her head on Esar-Haden's chest. "Tell me again, from the beginning."

Savior/Destroyer

Esar-Haden leaned with his back against the wood paneling of the library wall—waiting as patiently as any dark elf could—as the wizard flipped through the pages of a book.

Diffuse light filtered through twin windows at the end of the room. A chandelier hung above the table, flickering magical orbs of light in place of candles. Magical effects greeted him at every turn. Doors opened and closed without being touched. Feather dusters darted, leaving quick-fading sparkles in their wake. Even dirty dishes marched themselves to the kitchen, spilling not a crumb.

Esar-Haden, on being directed through the mansion by a man-servant in impressive livery, saw no other servants. "Do the linens launder themselves?" he asked his guide. He received no answer.

In the next chamber four women practiced a choral piece. Their harmony drew Esar-Haden's attention away from the annoyed searching of the wizard, a surface elf, who, with a word of magic, yanked free a massive tome from a nearby shelf. The book flew to a halt above the table then floated to a rest before the wizard, opening as it did so.

"Oltropp," the elven wizard glanced from the book to the dark elf, "that despicable halfling," he looked back down at the open pages before him, "says you're the best." His tone indicated disbelief or accusation, Esar-Haden couldn't tell which. In the adjoining room the women stopped their song and began to converse on the finer points of their craft.

"Sisters?" asked Esar-Haden, indicating the women with a point of his thumb at the closed door. The elven wizard looked up from his book.

"Mother and sisters," he said. "Your employer, head of the thieves' guild, Oltropp. You remember him, don't you?"

Esar-Haden could only imagine that when that clever halfling suggested a dark elf for the job, his client, a surface elf, bristled. Such a reaction would have amused Oltropp, who was chiefly concerned with entertaining himself.

Esar-Haden looked at the wizard. "Can you afford the best?"

"Humph! You must have crawled out of a profoundly deep gutter if you can't recognize fantastic wealth when you see it."

Esar-Haden pushed himself off the wall and strolled to the door. The women had begun the song anew and he wanted to hear it unmuffled by the wood, walls, and books. The door did not open. He sighed and without turning answered the elf. "The deepest, my sun-drenched cousin." He turned to face the wizard and smiled.

The wizard also smiled. "This amuses you, doesn't it? A rich and powerful surface elf, a wizard, no less, turning to a dark elf thug for help?"

"I'm easily amused." Esar-Haden walked to a plush chair across from the table and sat down. The wizard's face crinkled in annoyance. "The idea of a thieves' guild," continued Esar-Haden, "is a little silly, don't you think? If it weren't for the fact that we have to pool our gold to pay off government officials we would all be stabbing each other in the backs. It's the greater threat that preserves us."

The elven wizard frowned. "What was your name again?"

"Esar-Haden."

"Esar-Haden, I'm not concerned with the details of your profession, such as it is. I care about a scroll titled the

Chronicle of Mozer Qoth, a new acquisition at the Tower of Seven Gales."

Esar-Haden produced a thin throwing dagger from the interior of his left shirt sleeve and began to pick at his teeth. If he were lucky enough to meet any of the wizard's sisters he didn't want the remnants of lunch greeting them when he smiled. He wished the wizard had etiquette enough to offer him a glass of wine to swish around in his mouth. He glanced in the air about him, thinking that perhaps one floated nearby and he had failed to notice.

"Perhaps you aren't taking this seriously—"

"A smash and grab then?" interrupted Esar-Haden, turning back to the wizard.

"Smash and grab?" The wizard walked around the table and sat in the other upholstered chair. "My dear darkness dwelling *cousin.* In my time at the Tower of Seven Gales there were no fewer than," he held up four fingers, "break in attempts. One clever thief even attempted to pull down a section of wall with a golem he had somehow gotten control of."

Esar-Haden re-sleeved his dagger.

The elven wizard sat back, putting his fingertips together. "One thief was turned to stone. I believe he's still in the same spot, as a deterrent. Another was teleported to the Nine Hells. The golem-commanding thief was devoured by a swarm of fiendish centipedes. The golem?" He smiled. "Is gainfully employed. I can't recall what happened to the fourth but I can only assume they met with a horrible end."

"Soft entry, then?" concluded Esar-Haden.

"I can see by the look on your face that you're thoroughly confused." The wizard rose and returned to his books.

"I can do a soft entry," said Esar-Haden. "I'm the best, after all. It's just that I stick out due to the rarity of dark elves on the surface, also, my race is near-universally despised, so I'm not usually the go-to-guy for a confidence scam, seduction scam, or similar techniques."

The singing stopped. The wizard looked to the door. It swooshed open, revealing one of his sisters.

"Brother, you asked for me?"

Esar-Haden stood and turned to face the speaker.

Like her brother, her hair was long and light brown, blonde in places. She had well-shaped eyebrows over large pale green eyes that slanted at the corners. Her face tapered to a small chin, her nose was well shaped. A smattering of freckles gave her an air of child-like charm. She smiled demurely, revealing perfectly level teeth under well proportioned lips. She had white flowers woven into her hair. A pair of emerald earrings hung from her ears.

"My apologies. I didn't know you had a guest." She bowed and retreated from the room. As the door closed her eyes flashed, meeting Esar-Haden's, keeping them until the door broke the connection.

"Well mannered."

The wizard frowned. "I can only imagine the type of women that you're used to."

"Every type."

This brought a chuckle from the wizard. He stood and crossed his arms. The book he was reading closed itself. "I can't get into the details here. All I can tell you at this juncture is that you and I will gain entry to the Tower of Seven Gales. I will distract those who need distracting. You will sneak into the archives, deal with any obstacles, locate the *Chronicle,* and steal it. I will meet you later and we will conclude our transaction."

"Is that when I get devoured by fiendish centipedes?"

The wizard smirked. "If so, wouldn't Oltropp and the other thieves make it their lives' work to kill me?"

"It's the greater threat that preserves us."

"Are you up to it?"

"I'll have to gather a few things before we depart."

The wizard was pleased and went back to his books. Esar-Haden turned and began to leave but the wizard called after him. "I have to be sure." Esar turned. The surface elf looked him full in the face. "If murder becomes necessary—"

Esar-Haden laughed.

The wizard smiled, nodding his head. "Meet me in the back garden tomorrow at high noon. I know your kind love the sun. It will be amusing to watch you sweat and stumble around blindly."

Esar-Haden didn't feel the need to respond. He could find his own way out of the mansion. He assumed the right doors would open, the wrong ones stay shut. As he passed gaudy statues and overly-lacquered woodwork he wondered what the wizard had meant by, "obstacles."

. . .

The garden was a quilt of yellow, orange, and pink pastels, criss-crossed with ribbons of rose-colored stepping stones. The air shimmered with a rainbow of reflected color. The mingled scents of the flowers radiated out—a welcoming invitation. Esar-Haden arrived at the garden earlier than the appointed time. She surprised him when she spoke.

"You must not be used to such displays." Her hair was done up in elaborate braids. Her pale green eyes regarded him. She wore a simple muslin blouse and workman's trousers. She held a pair of sheers in her delicate fingers. The flesh of her bare arms was pale and as flawless as the petals of her well-tended flowers.

"Such beauty is rare." He meant her beauty, of course, and she caught his meaning, smiling in response.

He couldn't help but smile in return. He scanned the garden. "Your work?"

"All of us," she answered. "My mother and sisters, that is. My brother is far too busy, although," she looked to a corner of the garden. "He does grow some things he needs for spells."

"Your father?"

She looked from the flowers to the man who stood dangerously close to her (he was a dark elf, after all, and armed, his twin daggers hanging from his belt), shielding his eyes. "In the capital."

"I see," said Esar-Haden. "A wizard, like your brother?"

She looked at him, studying him, with such innocent curiosity it made him blush, not something he often did. "Yes."

"In the caves I grew up in, there were no flowers like these," he said. "The surface above was rock and sand. Although there was the occasional desert rose."

"A cave?" She tilted her head. "I couldn't imagine it. How gray and drab."

"Oh?" said Esar-Haden. "Nature took her time sculpting the caves, and she hid subtle beauty within. There are massive stalagmites, which the imagination shapes into fantastic brutes. There are cathedrals of soda straws. Pools of water so clear and still you would never know they were present, unless you broke their surface. In the desert sky above, the stars wrap around you, embracing you in their eternal mystery." He worried he was laying it on a bit thick but he had gotten carried away.

As Esar-Haden spoke she studied him. "You're not at all what I imagined."

"Ever meet a dark elf?"

"No," she said, "I'm afraid of them."

"You should be."

"Should I be afraid of you?"

"Certainly," he said, "but not today. Today I'm in awe of your garden," he looked at her, "and of your beauty." A few moments of silence passed as Esar-Haden admired the garden and the gardener.

She watched him with unabashed curiosity. "My brother told me about you."

Esar-Haden looked at her. "Oh? What does your brother know about me?"

"He says that it's rare for a dark elf to leave the darkness below. He says that makes you—different."

Esar-Haden shrugged his shoulders. "I suppose."

"He says that you're more virtuous than you pretend."

Esar-Haden couldn't help but chuckle.

"My brother says that you were born with a bright soul. He says you could have been an artist or a poet. But the culture you grew up in would have tried to kill that part of you. He wonders if those elements are hidden away, waiting for someone to make you feel safe, so that part of you can return."

Esar-Haden watched her as she spoke. She had a strange look in her eyes, as if she was already infatuated with the idealized, romantic figure she was defining. 'Why the hell is he feeding her all this non-sense?' He wondered. 'She was probably pestering him about my presence. He had to tell her something. He wasn't going to tell her the truth.' He thought it best to play along. "If we can find time, I will recite some of my poetry for you." Not that he had any poetry.

She smiled. "I would enjoy that. I could put it to music, if you like."

Esar-Haden smiled.

A noise came from the house, interrupting them. It was the door. She turned and looked. "My brother."

"What's your name?" asked Esar-Haden, before she could run. She turned back to him with a skittish look on her face. No doubt she had never imagined giving her name, or wanting to give her name, to a dark elf.

"Esmé." She moved past him, making her way out of the garden.

Esar-Haden heard the wizard's boots click on the stone pathway. He turned to face his new employer. The sun was at its apex. He had to shield his eyes, which watered without mercy due to the sun's light.

"Fall in love?" asked the wizard. Esar-Haden didn't answer. "You scared her, poor child. She's sheltered, you know? She no doubt has an instinctual distrust of your kind."

"One would hope."

The wizard reached out and touched Esar-Haden's arm. "You look miserable. Is it the sun?" He walked past Esar-Haden. "Ready?"

"How long is our journey? I forgot to ask."

The wizard had a good laugh at that. "Quaint." He paused to check the assorted spell component pouches about his person. "'Tis but a pleasant stroll in the sun, my tortured darkness dweller." He seemed satisfied with his cataloging and began walking. "Come."

The pair passed from the garden, heading down a gentle slope toward a large stand of oaks. The wild grasses grew to shoulder height. A cut path wove through the wilderness. At their approach small birds took flight.

"We'll teleport to a spot nearby," said the elven wizard. "Teleporting into the tower itself is impossible."

"Teleportation?" asked Esar-Haden. As he spoke, a glimpse of movement caught his eye. At first he took it for the grass yet it moved apart from that swaying motion. He watched out of the corners of his eyes, not wanting to give away that he had caught the movement. Her light brown hair mingled with the pale yellows of the grasses. Her off-white shirt provided just enough contrast to give her away. She was paralleling them.

The wizard looked over his shoulder at the dark elf. "Ever done it?"

Esar-Haden shook his head. "Still trying to figure out horses."

The wizard looked ahead. "You really are a fish out of water."

Esar-Haden ignored him. His eyes were on Esmé. She wove through the grass with ease, staying just out of her brother's peripheral vision. Esar-Haden looked at her, caught her attention, smiled, and winked. This drew a shy smile from her.

"You'll have to be patient," said the wizard, "while I scry to make sure we don't teleport into certain death."

"Seems reasonable," said Esar-Haden.

Esmé wasn't close enough to hear their words, not above the increasing breeze that now brought the loose strands of her hair into her face. She kept most of her attention on picking her footing, but she looked to Esar-Haden, afraid she would lose sight of him.

'She doesn't seem worried for her brother's safety, even with a dark elf at his back. She's curious about this exotic creature that's entered her sanctuary. What is this monstrous beetle on the delicate petals of your flower?'

He was not ignorant of the romance of it. He knew people were drawn to contrast. As the pair approached the forest Esmé darted from the grass into the trees. Esar-Haden lost sight of her. 'I should have my wits about me,' he chastised himself. 'Not be fawning over some female.'

The grass gave way to a tight clumping of trees. The wizard snaked his way through them, trailing Esar-Haden behind him. Not far into the forest the wizard came to a stop. Esar-Haden stepped up next to him. The wizard sat down with his legs crossed, closed his eyes, and began to meditate.

Esar-Haden heard her moving closer. He turned to see her break from the shifting light and shadow of the deep wood into the foreground. She caught his gaze and stopped. She darted behind a tree, taking partial cover from him. She stuck her head out and looked. He stepped closer, closing the gap.

Near the tree she hid behind stood a moss-covered obelisk. A large rough-cut emerald was embedded in the stone. It pulsed with a dull inner light. Esar-Haden scanned the area, spotting a second stone, then a third.

'I should have paid more attention to Soléne when she tried to teach me magic.' He laughed at himself. He hadn't thought about Soléne in some time. Memories of her were always bittersweet. 'Still, the few spells she taught me have made all the difference.'

Esmé stepped out from behind a tree. Esar-Haden looked at her. She clung to it for a moment, then stepped out in front of the tree, despite her insecurity. She reached up with one hand and pulled the strands of hair from her eyes. The emeralds in the stones pulsed. The light was echoed in the gems of her earrings, illuminating the slender curve of her neck.

Esar-Haden stepped toward her, saw her tense like a jackrabbit ready to take flight, and stopped his advance. 'Sure is a skittish thing,' he thought. He stepped back two steps, to where he had started. She smiled. 'She wants to come to me,' he thought, 'Or come almost to me, then have me pounce on her.'

Esar-Haden glanced over his shoulder at the wizard. He sat motionless, moving his lips without sound. Esar-Haden looked back to Esmé. She pulled away from the tree and stepped forward. She stood now on her own, not hiding or bracing herself against anything. The green glow of the emeralds fell on the pale skin of her forearms. Esar-Haden was captivated by her curious behavior. He watched and waited for her to either approach or disappear into the woods. Instead, she stood there, gazing at him.

"Esar?" The wizard spoke as if from a dream. At the sound of her brother's voice, Esmé crouched behind a thickly-leafed bush. Esar-Haden turned and looked at the wizard. "Esar?" repeated the wizard, reaching his hand out, searching for the dark elf.

"Here," said Esar-Haden, stepping up.

"Ready?" asked the wizard, his voice a whisper.

"Always."

The wizard began to chant, sparkles of magic falling from his fingertips as he drew a complex pattern in the air. His eyes opened but they were rolled back and the pupils could not be seen. Esar-Haden looked for Esmé. He saw her peering through the leaves of the bush. The thin streams of light cutting through the leaves began to twist and coil. The wizard's voice rose. Esmé leapt from the bushes, spinning away from the pair.

Everything went white.

. . .

The ground beneath Esar-Haden shifted, his feet sliding several inches before finding purchase. Dark shapes materialized as his vision returned. His hands went to his daggers. He was mollified when the looming shapes were revealed to belong to the pine trees surrounding him. Motion to his left caught his attention. The elven wizard was rising to his feet.

The pair stood in a small clearing. Pine trees hid everything else from view. The ground was a carpet of needles. At the sudden arrival of two new occupants in the grove a startled squirrel began to click its teeth. After a moment's protest it ran up the branch to cover.

"See, Esar-Haden, nothing to it." The wizard turned to face him. "Over there," he said, motioning with a limp finger, "although you can't see it, is the Tower of Seven Gales. Surrounding the tower is, of course, the town of Seven Gales." The wizard knocked the pine needles from his backside. "And inside the tower is the *Chronicle of Mozer Qoth*." He thought for a moment before continuing.

"The Tower is no grand palace. It's small and cramped. It was built by an eccentric old wizard named Seruli. He was more fond of books than people. So you can imagine what consideration he gave to living quarters. That's to our advantage. Most of the wizards who haunt the library during the day retire to their own homes in the town at night. There remains, however, a rotation of two wizards who live in the tower itself. They have the glorious job of keeping watch should anyone break in, or attempt it.

"It's not a bad position. I've held it myself. You get free run of the library. I happen to know who one of these two is, a man named Edward Heath. I know this because Edward and I have been enjoying a little romance through steamy letters written with a quickened pulse, if you catch my meaning."

"Ah, seduction," said Esar-Haden.

"That's right, and it's been playing out over a long enough timespan to be quite effective. Edward is salivating for me. He knows full well I'm unattainable. That makes it all the more tantalizing for him. He knows that I'm not allowed in the tower upon penalty of death. He knows that ours is a romance that can never be fulfilled. At least not until he leaves the tower."

"Or until you show up and declare that you can't wait," said Esar-Haden, "that you're willing to risk death to have him in your arms."

"Me in his," said the wizard, with nonchalance. "He will feel a masculine pride at having drawn me to him. He will feel the need to protect me from the dangers of being caught, from the injustice of my banishment. He will draw me in at once, as an act of principled rebellion."

"And to consummate—"

"That is none of your concern," snapped the wizard.

"Ah, the seduction scam, always double-edged."

"All you know is a knife at an unprotected throat," said the elven wizard. "If you knew what the *Chronicle* was, if you had any idea what secrets are locked away, hidden in Mozer's mad scribbles, what it can do, what you could do with it," the elf laughed, "you would rent yourself out like the filthiest brothel whore just to get a glance at it."

Esar-Haden raised a skeptical eyebrow.

"Those fools have no idea," said the wizard, looking toward the Tower. The wizard stepped away from Esar-Haden. "I'll bring down the protective spells, open the door, and let you in. You know what to do from there."

"The second wizard?"

"That's your problem. Can you handle this or have I made a mistake?"

"Wizards are easy. As long as they don't see you coming, giving them time to catch you in their magic tricks, they're helpless."

The wizard smiled. "That kind of thinking will get you killed."

"When the scroll goes missing, won't you be found out?" asked Esar-Haden. "I mean, why would either of the two wizards take the fall if they don't have to? Won't they pin it on you?"

"Edward Heath comes from a rich and politically powerful family. His reputation and political ties are what gained him access to the tower, not his talent as a wizard. He has little of that. To even accuse him would cost the tower dearly. If they did accuse him there's no chance he would mention my name. Edward's sexuality is quite private. No, the fact that I had been at the tower will never come to light."

"Whomever this other wizard is, I feel sorry for him," said Esar-Haden, although he wasn't genuinely concerned for the fate of this second, unknown wizard. "Either I'll kill him," said Esar-Haden, "or he'll take the fall." He looked at the elven wizard. "Does your conscience bother you?"

The wizard smirked. "Come to the tower well after the sun has gone down, and the town is asleep. Keep hidden, oh, and," his smiled grew sinister, "watch out for the golem."

"Looks like I'm hanging out here for the rest of the day," said Esar-Haden, looking around at the pines.

"No, that won't do. What if someone else teleports in? They'll scry and spot you. You'll have to find somewhere in the countryside or in town to hide. You're a professional, should be easy. Maybe there's a local thieves' guild. You could make new friends." The wizard turned and started through the pines, giggling at his own joke. Although he disappeared from sight, his laugh lingered.

Esar-Haden sighed and began to take the same path as the wizard when he heard panicked breathing. He drew his daggers and spun, searching for the source. He didn't have to search hard to find her. She was frantically sliding side-to-side before the stone wall that surrounded the teleportation spot, her hands on it, feeling it, as if her mind couldn't comprehend it was there.

Esar-Haden re-sheathed his daggers. He stepped up to her. He was right next to her yet she didn't notice him. She stared at the wall, blinking as rapidly as she was breathing. Her face was florid. Esar-Haden reached out and placed a hand on her shoulder. "Esmé." She turned her head and looked at him—eyes wide with fear. She blinked, turned to look at the wall, then turned back to him. "You've been teleported."

Esmé reached up and placed her hand over Esar-Haden's. She stood this way for some time, blinking, staring straight ahead at neither him nor the wall, but into the shadows between the pines. Esar-Haden watched her. Esmé whispered.

"Say again."

Esmé looked up at him. "My brother—you—"

Esar-Haden frowned. "You heard?"

"I—" She was cognizant of her hand on his, of their touch, of her disgust. She jerked away from him. "My brother a thief! You a—" she looked away from him, "murderer."

Esar-Haden crossed his arms.

She turned to face him. "How can my brother do this? You must have—"

"Power corrupts."

"Power corrupts?"

Esar-Haden uncrossed his arms. "I don't mean to be flippant, but, yes, it does." He stepped toward her. She didn't backpedal, as he expected. "Imagine having the power to shape reality. Imagine knowing the secret language of the gods."

She studied him with a mixture of horror and curiosity on her face.

"Once you got an ounce of that," he said, "what wouldn't you do for a pound?"

"I wouldn't—" she said, her voice breaking as she began to cry.

Esar-Haden reached out, caressed her cheek, freeing a teardrop from her soft skin. She pulled away from his touch. He looked at the bead of water on the tip of his finger. "Maybe," he looked at her, "you wouldn't be corrupted."

"Esar," she spoke in a soft tone, "you have to stop him." She reached out and took his wrist. She lowered his hand and put her own hand within, locking her fingers with his. "My brother, he isn't thinking clearly. He can't want this, not truly. This isn't our family. We weren't raised to hurt others."

Esar-Haden looked down at their hands. He looked into her face. The pleading look in her eyes, begging for a morality he lacked, made him feel dirty. He frowned, pulled his hand free, and turned away.

"Your brother said you were sheltered," he turned back, "you have what some might call a perfect life. Your innocence has been kept whole. Your mind has remained untroubled by the violence of everyday living. Despite what you might think of me, I do understand, at least to a degree, how a person like you thinks, how you perceive the world. I'm sorry to be the first to strike against your innocence but your brother is going to—"

"Kill? For a piece of paper?" asked Esmé. "Why? Life gives you everything you need to be happy." She took his hand, interlocked their fingers once more, and squeezed.

Esar-Haden frowned. "Maybe life gave *you* everything—" The look in her tear-filled eyes gave him pause. "Listen, we've got to find a hole to hide in. We're not safe here."

Esmé released his hand, stiffened her jaw, and planted her feet. "I'm going to find my brother and stop him."

"Esmé, I don't think you know your brother—"

"I know him better than you do. I'll talk him out of it."

"Once he finds out you know of his plans," said Esar-Haden, "he'll kill you."

Her features changed from defiance to shock. "He would never!"

Esar-Haden couldn't help but chuckle. "The only option now is to keep you hidden and get you back home the way you got here, teleported, with your brother ignorant of your presence. That's the only way you're staying alive."

She wanted to protest but caught herself. She realized she was talking to a dark elf, a mercenary, thief, and contract killer in the employ of her brother. If her brother had gone this far, could he be talked out of going all the way, she asked herself. She began to doubt that her brother would react in the way she assumed he would; that is, seeing the error of his way, falling to his knees with grief over the condition of his soul, and begging her and the gods for forgiveness. The danger and precariousness of her situation became clear.

Esar-Haden watched this all unfold on her face. "You'll have to live with the knowledge," he said. "But at least you'll live."

He turned and started through the pines. After a few steps he turned and offered his hand to her. "Come on." She looked at him for a long time before moving. She passed him without taking his hand.

. . .

Esar-Haden stopped her at the gate. He opened it and looked out. The town of Seven Gales was nestled in a valley beneath them. A field of alfalfa extended down the slope of the hill. Cows and horses meandered and fed. A walking path led from the hill to the town. Trees were scattered here and there but no grouping was deep enough to provide a secure place to hide.

"Let's look around," he said, trying to take her hand, but she pulled away from him—she followed him, nonetheless. He kept to the wall, circling around. He saw what he suspected was a creek lined by a thick ribbon of trees a short walk away. He headed toward it, Esmé behind him. Luckily, no farmhand spotted them.

He found a comfortable spot in the shade close to the creek and sat down. Esmé stood a few feet away. Esar-Haden searched his pockets. He pulled free a packet of smoked meat and bit off a chunk. He held it out to Esmé. She crossed her arms and turned her head.

"It's going to be a while. You might as well get comfortable." He reached into his pack and produced a wineskin, uncorked it, took a sip, then offered this to his unhappy companion.

Esmé found her obstinance a bit silly. After all, she asked herself, what else could she do but trust him. She sat down next to Esar-Haden, facing him. She took both the jerky and the wine.

"I don't often eat meat."

"I got a few pears. Want one?"

"Yes, please," she said, handing back the jerky.

Esar-Haden was digging through his pack in search of the pears when she asked, "Does that hurt?"

Esar-Haden tried to figure out what she was asking about but couldn't.

"That." She reached out and pointed at his neck.

"Oh, my tattoo." He chuckled. "It did hurt, not any more." He wiped the pear on his sleeve and handed it to her.

"What did it feel like?" She bent forward and began to trace the letters with the tip of her finger. She caught herself and pulled away. Her cheeks blushed with embarrassment.

"It felt like I was getting my throat cut."

"How did they do it?"

"Eh," he chuckled, "you don't want to know."

They sat for a while eating, taking sips from the wineskin, and listening to the fish splashing in the creek.

"Three of you?" asked Esar-Haden.

"Three of—"

"I mean, sisters. I was just thinking that I have three sisters and I wonder if he did too."

"Oh, yes, there are."

"How funny," said Esar-Haden. "We've both got three sisters but otherwise our lives couldn't be more different."

"Except you're both thieves."

He turned and looked at her, studying her expression. "Oh, yeah, that too." Again a few minutes of silence passed. "You said that your father is a wizard in the city? Judging from your family's wealth he must be a powerful man."

"Yes, I suppose he is," she sighed. "He's been in the capital most of my life. He serves the people, he says. That leaves little time for us. Oh," she added, "I know he's an important man, a good man, even, but—" Her voice fell away into silence.

Esar-Haden studied her. "I didn't know my father, either," he said, "or my mother."

She looked at him. "Who raised you?"

"No one, really. My sister, Yolandi, if you could call her abuse 'raising.' Then, the streets of Pwyll, the dark elf city I'm from."

"An orphan?"

Esar-Haden laughed. "All male dark elves are orphans of a sort. You see, in dark elf society in general, and especially in Pwyll, the males are considered inferior. This leads to all sorts of transgressions against us. Some males have it better, some worse. Anyway, I had a home to go to, a place to sleep, that is. But I spent as much time as possible in the Ghetto of White Skin, running with kids like me—throw aways."

"That's sad, Esar."

"It's been interesting, to say the least."

"My brother—" began Esmé, but stopped short. She sorted her thoughts and continued. "I think he's always felt like he could never equal our father's achievements. Even when he was a boy he drove himself relentlessly, as if trying to catch up to our father—or outrun his inner demons." She shook her head. "He never played as a child." She glanced at Esar-Haden. "He's never sang with us. He's always been—" She looked down. "And now this." She looked at him. "He frightens me. I fear what you said is true, that if I tried to stop him he would kill me." She trembled and tears fell to her cheeks. "I'm scared."

Esar-Haden scooted close to her and wrapped a comforting arm around her shoulder.

"By this time tomorrow, you'll be tending to your beautiful garden."

She looked at him. "What if you get killed?"

"Hey," he smiled and squeezed her, "that's no way to think."

"Are you really going to kill that other wizard?"

"I'm going to slip by him like a shadow. Despite what I told your bother, it's not smart to fight a wizard if you don't have to."

"What will he do with it? I mean—"

"The, what did he call it, the *Chronicle*?" Esar-Haden removed his arm from around Esmé. "Who knows? Half the time wizards think in grand schemes but then reality intercedes. He said they're mad scribbles. I bet they don't make a damn bit of sense." He smiled. "That's why I prefer gold. I know I can spend it. Never any doubt about that."

She chuckled, then sighed, then looked up at the sky through the leaves above. She looked at him, studying his face. She reached, lifted his arm, and returned it to her shoulder, leaning into him. "We've got time, you promised to recite some of your poetry."

"Yeah," he laughed. "About that."

. . .

Esar-Haden woke with a start. Esmé was still in his arms, asleep. Only a remnant of the sun's rays remained. The shade had become shadow. A chill came over Esar-Haden, causing him to shiver. He pulled the blanket from his bedroll tighter around their tangled forms.

Esmé awoke and shivered, wrapping her arms tighter around him. "Can we build a fire?"

"A little one," he said, rising. She rose too and in the semi-darkness they both dressed, both a bit shy, both a bit shocked at their quick and complete intimacy. He searched the area for fallen branches. She watched him break and assemble the branches and twigs. He stuffed dried leaves beneath them then produced a tinderbox from his pack.

"The sun's going down." She watched him light the fire and blow on the tiny flame. "I guess that means you're going to the tower?"

He looked at her. He knew that she didn't want him to go. "Stay here and keep warm," he said. "Wait maybe an hour or so, then hide in the same spot you found yourself in after being teleported. Wait there until your brother and I return. When your brother teleports us home, you sneak into your bedroom and pretend you've been there the entire time. Maybe I'll join you," he joked. She didn't laugh.

"Can you get the scroll without hurting anyone—or without getting hurt?" she asked. He didn't answer. She remained quiet for some time. The popping of sticks in the fire echoed through the trees. "What if my brother tries to kill you?"

"Why would he do that?"

"I don't know." She shook her head. "Silly thoughts. I'm just worried." She reached for him. He sat next to her and she wrapped her arms around him. "I didn't expect— I never—" She studied his face. "Don't do it. Don't go."

"I have to."

"No you don't."

"How are we going to get home without him?"

"I don't know. We'll find a way," she said. "Esar, I don't want you to get killed. In your arms I felt—"

He kissed her forehead. "I won't." He stood, breaking her hold on him. "Like a shadow, remember?" He saw that she wasn't comforted. "Esmé." She looked up at him. "I know what I'm doing." He glanced at the fire. "Keep warm. In an hour head out." He bent and cupped her chin. "In two hours I'll tuck you into bed."

. . .

Esar-Haden stood outside of the Tower of Seven Gales, gazing at what was once a thief, a second-story man, who hung from a windowsill above. He'd been turned to stone. Esar-Haden tried to see the man's face, but couldn't.

'This is where your career ended,' he thought, studying the second-story man. He worried that his might end here as well. He reached out and patted the stone thief on the rump. 'I've got an inside guy.' The thought did not mollify his fear.

He walked around the tower. When he got to the front door he stopped. A ball of blue-white light hung above the door, floating in space, attached to nothing—magical fumes held it aloft. Esar-Haden stood just at the edge of the pool of light, feet set wide, hands resting on the pommels of his daggers.

A few minutes passed. He heard movement and slid his hands down over the handles of his daggers. He turned his head so he could hear. He heard nothing more, saw nothing. A sound from the opposite direction came to him—the door latch. Esar-Haden pulled one of his daggers free. The door opened and the slender frame of the elven wizard leaned against the jam. "Well," said the elven wizard, "here we are."

Esar-Haden sheathed his dagger and stepped close to the wizard, placing his hand on the door. The wizard stepped backwards into the interior of the tower, allowing Esar-Haden to enter, then shut the door. Only the light of the moon, falling through tall windows in lazy silver arcs, illuminated the space.

Standing in an alcove that once held a bookshelf was a stone statue of a warrior. Even though it appeared as nothing more than a bit of impressive statuary, it held the promise of movement and possessed an air of menace. The elven wizard noticed Esar-Haden studying it. "The aforementioned golem. Ever see one?"

"Nope," said Esar-Haden.

"Don't worry," said the elven wizard. "Followed?"

"Not possible," said Esar-Haden. "Point me to the archives."

"Down the hall," said the elven wizard, motioning with his head. "Take the stairs down until you can go no further."

"And then?"

"And then—" The wizard grinned, turned, and started up a rough-cut stone staircase.

Esar-Haden watched him disappear into darkness. He turned and headed down the hall, daggers in hand.

. . .

Esar-Haden stopped at the end of the hall before a partially opened door. The crackle of a torch could be heard. A stone staircase descended in a spiral. A torch burned in a holder a few feet away, throwing yellow-orange washes onto the blue-grey stone. There were torches in wall holders every ten feet, offering just enough light to annoy him. He preferred near total darkness; by which, like a cat, he could see remarkably well.

He was moving as cautiously and silently as he could. He was listening, his acute dark elf ears on alert. It was this focus that brought the sound of rustling fabric to his awareness. A second after, the light from behind him dimmed: someone or something was moving in front of the torch.

Esar-Haden turned and steadied himself on the stairs. 'Great spot for an ambush,' he cursed. 'He even has the high ground. Still, I might have the element of surprise.'

A figure came into view on the stairs. Whoever it was, they were wrapped in a dark cloak, pulled shut. The cowl was down and Esar-Haden could see nothing of the individual, except for long, strait, blood-red hair spilling out of the cowl's opening. Esar-Haden didn't want to allow the cloak to open and a wand or a raised finger sprouting lightening to emerge. He lunged upwards and thrust his main hand dagger into the center of the cloak.

He felt no resistance. He tried to draw his hand back for a second strike but before he could the cloaked figure dissolved into black smoke. Esar-Haden thought he recognized the peculiar smell that came with the smoke, but he couldn't place it. The smoke curled around him, enveloped him, then spread thin until it disappeared.

'Either I met the second wizard just now or something even worse is going on.' He stood with his back against the stone wall, looking up and down the stairs, listening, waiting. Nothing came. Not a sound except for the crackling of the torches. 'No going back now,' he told himself. He took a few deep breaths and continued down the stairs.

The stairs ended in a hall. It twisted and turned for seemingly no reason other than to frustrate him. His sixth sense told him something was coming. He pressed himself into a turn in the hall and waited. He heard the click of heels on stone.

A black-stocking leg curled around the corner, ending in a mirror-polished stiletto heel. The leg slid to the ground, pulled its owner forward, into view, then disappeared into the rich, textured black cloth of a cloak.

The cloak was pulled around her, the hood up. She had her head bent, the cloth hid her face. Her blood-red hair spilled from the opening. This time Esar-Haden could detect her voluptuous curves, even under the cloak. Again the familiar smell came but again he couldn't recall where he had come across it before.

"A nice trick," he said, "the poof of smoke routine." She made no reply. She kept to the opposite side of the narrow hall, still advancing. Her stocking legs and black heels flashed in and out of the open front of the cloak. Esar-Haden leveled his off-hand dagger in front of him, defensively. He pulled the main hand dagger down to his waist, ready to strike with it. "Going to risk it again?"

The cloaked figure did not lift her head, did not reveal herself. She was close enough for him to strike. Still, she did not slow her approach. As she passed she reached out. Her hand was gloved in black satin, extending all the way to her elbow. Esar-Haden tensed. She traced the edge of his dagger's blade with one finger. Esar-Haden swore he heard her purr. She withdrew her hand and pulled the cloak shut. She spun, the cloak twirling and began to walk back the way she'd came. Within seconds she was around the bend, gone from view.

He hadn't expected an obstacle quite like this. He followed her. For a moment he had the suspicion he himself was being followed. He didn't hear a sound, however. He chalked it up to a growing sense of paranoia.

He kept on the trail of the voluptuous, cloaked entity. The hall had so many bends and turns he could hardly keep sight of her. He could only catch the black cloak as it disappeared around corners.

'What are you doing?' he asked himself. 'You're an idiot to follow her. You told Esmé you knew what you were doing but this is amateur stuff.' He berated himself. 'You know you're walking into a trap. Turn around, find Esmé, and get out of here!' Yet, even as he thought it, he knew he wasn't going to turn back. He was too damned curious. Besides, mysterious female or no, he had a job to do, and he was just stupid enough to persist.

The mysterious, cloaked female led him into a natural cavern. In the center of the cavern was a stone dais. Situated on this dais was a circular mattress piled high with furs. Once in the chamber, the cloaked figure turned to face him, drawing back the hood. The features of her face were perfect, too perfect.

She had red-painted lips, high cheekbones, and large dark eyes framed in smoky-red. Esar-Haden frowned when he saw the small horns protruding from her forehead. He knew a demon when he saw one. He realized the familiar smell—brimstone. He had smelled it in Maljamir, the deepest of the trio of caves that made up Pwyll—the cave inhabited by demons. Although he knew what she was, his eyes couldn't stop exploring. She knew they couldn't. She flung her cloak open so he could continue.

A leather under-bust corset thrust her breasts forward. She wore a short, black leather skirt. Her hips curved dramatically. A pair of crimson, featherless wings extended from her back.

The succubus let the cloak fall to the floor. She advanced, her heels clicking, until she stood in front of Esar-Haden. She was a foot taller than he was. She looked down at him. Her wings extended, wrapping around him, situating the pair in their own private space. Esar-Haden knew what she could do. He knew how dangerous she was. He also knew that his daggers, not being heavily enough enhanced with magic, couldn't even break her skin. He sheathed them.

"I'm looking for a scroll."

"No scrolls here." She reached out and traced a finger along his jawline, licking her blood-red lips as she did so.

"You wouldn't mind if I poked around in the corners just to be sure?" Esar-Haden reached up and pressed against her wing, hoping to find his way out of her demonic embrace.

"Do you find me attractive?" Her voice slithered into his head. He felt the compulsion to compliment her, to feed her ego, to please her—to worship her. He knew it was part of her power. He fought it. A halting, choking laughter came from somewhere outside of the winged enclosure. Esar-Haden looked into the succubus's enchanting eyes.

"Friend of yours?"

"Lover."

"Ah."

Her wings pressed against Esar-Haden's back, forcing his body against hers. He looked up. She bent her head and dragged her lips against his cheek. She kissed her way to his ear. "What's your name?" While she waited for an answer, she busied herself with biting his neck.

"Esar-Haden."

"Where did you come from, Esar-Haden?" She was kissing, biting, and sucking on the juncture where his neck met his jaw, just below his ear. He felt his temperature rising.

"Pwyll."

She pulled back and looked at him, recognition in her eyes.

"Heard of it?"

"Maljamir?" she asked. Esar-Haden nodded. Her shapely lips turned into a frown. "You're one of the Sidonai?"

"That's right," said Esar-Haden.

"You're a long way from home, Sidonai." She narrowed her eyes. "A long way from your masters."

"Perhaps," said Esar-Haden, his smile turning into a firm line. The succubus retracted her wings. Esar-Haden became aware of a short, twisted body next to his. He glanced over at the man. Her "lover" stood no more than five feet tall, due to painful-looking contortions of his bones and musculature. The man's head was bulbous; the features of his face were shoved to one side. A second face, infantile and placid, was scrunched next to the first. Esar-Haden shuddered and looked back to the much more pleasing body of the succubus.

The succubus turned and walked a few steps toward the dais before stopping. She looked over her shoulder at Esar-Haden, saw his eyes on her, and smiled. She arced her back and thrust out her hips.

"Lover," she said, her voice like silk. "Make the Sidonai *comfortable*."

"Yes, Mistress," said the jumbled, distorted, two-faced man. He crooked an arm and extended a finger. Esar-Haden went for a dagger but was too late. A black arc of energy shot from the man's gnarled finger. Esar-Haden screamed in pain and fell unconscious to the ground.

. . .

The smell of brimstone once again filled Esar-Haden's nostrils. He opened his eyes. He was lying on the rough stone of the cave floor, on his side. His hands were bound behind his back. His ankles were tied together. He could see that his belt and daggers were lying on the dais. The succubus was reclining on the furs, her dark eyes on him. She held a whip in her hand. It snaked down, traveling across her legs, curling up next to her black stiletto heels.

A second scent caught his attention. He recognized it. "Esmé!?" He looked around. She stumbled into view. "What—"

One of her eyes was starting to swell shut, her skin discolored from bruising, and there was fresh blood on her lips. She stopped, looked at him, then lunged forward, having been pushed. Her brother came into view, laughing. Esmé tried to rush forward, toward Esar-Haden, but her brother was quicker. He reached out and grabbed a fistful of hair, halting her.

"You—" yelled Esar-Haden. "What's she doing here?"

"She—" began the elven wizard.

"We're here for the scroll," interrupted Esar-Haden. "What's this—"

"Oh, Esar-Haden, how obtuse."

"Silence!" commanded the succubus, her voice rebounded around the cave. "These two are suitable for the ritual?"

"Yes, Mistress," answered the elven wizard. "A dark elf thief and murderer. Something evil and corrupt, as the ritual calls for and—" Esar-Haden could see the smile widening on his face. "An innocent, a virgin, something pure." He laughed. "My own sister."

"You bastard!" interjected Esar-Haden.

"You did exactly as I expected, sister," said the elven wizard, ignoring the dark elf's condemnation. "You took the bait—the ebony-skinned worm." He laughed, glancing at Esar-Haden. "When you felt the hook you panicked. Now you'll—"

"Brother! Please!" pleaded Esmé.

"Ugh. Enough of your whining," said the elven wizard. He shoved her down. She fell into a heap on the floor. "Stay!" he commanded. He approached the dais. "Mistress, may I?"

The succubus nodded. The elven wizard crawled on top of the furs, making his way to her. He curled up beside her and looked at the two fools he'd lured to their end, a smug, satisfied look on his face. "Have I done well, Mistress? Are you happy?"

"You brought me your own sister? A nice touch." He looked up into her face, just in time to see her smile turned to a frown. "There's just one problem." She pointed at Esar-Haden. "He's a Sidonai." The elven wizard looked confused.

"A Sidonai? I've never heard of—"

"He's spoken for," she said, "his soul—claimed by the fiends of Maljamir."

Esar-Haden watched the color drain from the elven wizard. He looked from Esar-Haden to the succubus. "I—"

"However," she interrupted. "A claim is only a claim. I possess him now and that's all that matters." At hearing this the elven wizard visibly relaxed.

"Are you sure about that?" asked Esar-Haden. "You don't want to piss off the wrong demonic lord."

The succubus shot him an angry glance. "It's too late for you." She looked to the two-faced man. "Seruli, draw the circle." She nudged the elven wizard. He guessed her will and slid from the dais.

He walked over to Esar-Haden, crouching next to him. "You said you were the best. Ha! Look at you." He reached out and moved Esar-Haden's white hair out of his face. "Did you like my little ruse? I worked hard on it. Like writing a fiction, you have to get every detail right. When Oltropp suggested—"

"Your own sister?" asked Esar-Haden.

The elf looked to the sobbing, pathetic form of his sister. "Demonic rituals are complicated, Esar-Haden. Any old human sacrifice won't do. The ritual we are going to perform today has *detailed* requirements."

"Listen to me," whispered Esar-Haden. "I know you're an arrogant prick, you think you can control everything. You're as smart as they come, aren't you?" The elven wizard smiled in response. Esar-Haden continued. "A succubus? A demonic ritual? You have no idea what you're getting yourself into. Believe me, I know."

The elven wizard seemed to be contemplating the dark elf's words. He leaned in close to Esar-Haden, "What's a Sidonai?"

"You think you're going to give me and your sister over to some demon and reap the rewards? It doesn't work that way. I'm not the price, I'm the bait, *you* pay the price."

"We'll see, Esar. Now, you'll have to excuse me. I should help Seruli, he has bad eyesight." With that the wizard rose and walked over to the hunched figure of the deformed man.

Esar-Haden turned to Esmé. "Psst," he whispered. She lifted her tear-streaked face from her hands and looked over to him. "Get out of here!" She blinked several times with her un-swollen eye, staring at him, not comprehending. "Esmé! You aren't tied up. Get the hell out of here."

"She's not going anywhere," said the succubus. "The poor thing is in shock. This is all too much for her fragile mind. Be quiet!" The succubus turned away from her captives and kept an eye on her lovers.

Esar-Haden watched as the circle was drawn. The deformed wizard held a copper pot in the crook of his left arm. He dipped his fingers into it and drew them out covered in blood. He bent awkwardly and sketched out the circle and magic runes on the floor, mumbling the necessary words as he did so. The elven wizard stood close to him, repeating the words.

When the circle was completed Seruli crossed the room raised his fingers to the flame of a torch. The blood on his fingers ignited, burning a blue-green. He shuffled back to the circle, bent once more, and lit the blood on the floor. The fire consumed the blood, leaving behind a sticky black residue.

"Excellent!" said the succubus. She looked to Esar-Haden and Esmé.

The two wizards approached.

"Esmé! Run!" Esar-Haden yelled, as he tried to scoot away from them. He didn't get far. Seruli grabbed his ankle and with a grunt began to drag him across the room. Esar tried to wiggle and fight, but there was little he could do. The elven wizard grabbed his own sister by the hair. He took visible relish in dragging her into the infernal diagram. Then both of them left the circle.

"Esmé," whispered Esar-Haden. "Untie me! Esmé, come on, girl, snap out of it." Esmé was slumped next to him, her eyes shut, her lithe frame shaken by her crying. "Esmé, please—"

The succubus laughed. "Look at the fierce dark elf killer beg a frightened child for help. You delight me, Esar-Haden."

"Esar?" whispered Esmé. Esar-Haden glanced toward the dais. Both Seruli and Esmé's brother were standing before the succubus, awaiting orders.

"Untie my wrists. Hurry."

"What's happening?" moaned Esmé. "Are we going to die?"

The succubus bent forward and grabbed Esar-Haden's belt. She stood and crossed the short distance between the dais and the ritual circle. Both of her lovers followed her. She crouched, hovering over both Esmé and Esar. "The Sidonai certainly are fearless," she mused. "Must be the few drops of demonic blood you've got swirling around in you." She rose, drew out one of Esar-Haden's daggers, and handed it to the elven wizard. "A souvenir." She flipped her hair and uncurled her wings. She tossed the belt and second dagger into the darkness at the edge of the cave. "Begin the ritual."

The wizards and the succubus took up their positions and began to chant.

Esar-Haden rolled over onto his other side so he could better communicate with Esmé.

"This thing's going to go horribly wrong," he whispered. "When it does—"

Before he could finish the hairs on his neck rose. The air became charged. A black ball, crawling with electricity, formed in the air above Esmé and him. The voices of the trio were soon lost in the crackling of energy. The ball expanded, first, slowly, then, in one frightening swell. The ball exploded in silence, filling the room with an inky darkness.

A slender figure could be seen. She hovered at the center of the magic circle, above and just to the side of Esar and Esmé. She was not only slender but small. It took a moment for Esar-Haden to realize it was a trick of perspective. She was far away, still locked in the Abyss, struggling to cross over. From what Esar-Haden could make out the demon was ebony-skinned, like him. Unlike him, she was wreathed in flames of scintillating, shifting colors.

The succubus saw her as well. "Syrryx, the Light in the Darkness," she said, her voice reverent. "She comes!"

The form of Syrryx grew larger and larger. The ritual was working. She was crossing over. Visibly, she still appeared to be a significant distance away, but her power projected forward, onto this plane.

"Yes." He heard her say. Her voice a whisper at his ear, a whisper devoid of the wet heat that belonged to it. "Your soul has black marks. Every life you've taken has left an indelible stain. You will be the salt, the bitter taste to offset the sweet. I will devour you last, to remind me of the sorrow of life."

Esar-Haden felt her touch leave him. The echo of her voice remained at his ear a moment longer. "I will devour her," there was a pause, "first. I will savor her innocence. She is the sweetness, purity, the absence of sin. The delicate flower of life."

Esar-Haden was looking into Esmé's face when the color drained from it. The cold touch was on her now. A scream filled the room, but not from Esmé. It was a scream that traveled across a great expanse of space. A scream that was so anguished it pained the occupants of the room to hear it.

The room was instantly filled with the angry hissing and crackling of electricity. It came from the darkness at the edges of the room and drove its way into the miniature form of Syrryx. She screamed in pain. It was the angry magic of a ritual gone wrong.

"No!" cried the succubus. "What's happening?" She looked back and forth between her lovers. "What's happening?"

The answer came from Syrryx, who screamed through the pain. "Impure!" A bolt of electricity silenced her. The distant demon hung in the air between worlds, held aloft on arcs of thick, white lightning. The succubus stood in shocked silence. She looked back and forth between Esar-Haden and Esmé. "What?" she asked, her voice barely audible above the popping and buzz of the electricity. She turned to the elven wizard. "You said—" But her words were stolen from her as the electricity curled downwards and reached between her breasts.

"Agh!" The elven wizard was struck rigid by a bolt of electricity. The single bolt was followed by several others, angry magic lashing out at its authors. Esar-Haden rolled over onto his other side. He searched for Seruli. He soon found the grotesque form of the wizard. He had been knocked to the floor, bolts of electricity pressing him down. Seruli's body convulsed, but it was clear he was dead.

Esar-Haden turned back over. He was about to speak when the electricity found its way to him. The first shock took his breath away. The second set his skin on fire, or so it felt. The magic leapt from him to Esmé. He watched, helplessly, as the electricity drove into her. Her muscles spasmed. She flopped and twisted. The electricity danced along her body, causing her to twirl over onto her other side. The flashing energy went elsewhere. Esar-Haden saw something white-hot glowing at her back. Something tucked into her belt.

Now the electricity converged on the demon mother, the Light in the Darkness. It blotted out the fire she wreathed herself in with its own angry color.

Esmé moved. She groped, touching herself, identifying the pain. Esar-Haden, disciplined by the harsh tortures of his youth, could control his reaction to pain. Still, it took him several seconds to find his voice.

"Esmé."

She moaned, but not in response to him. She was still lost in her pain. In the background Esar-Haden could hear the screaming of Syrryx. The sound was growing more and more distant, like a wounded animal howling as it ran away from its attacker.

Esar-Haden tried to scan the room but the blinding white column of energy was right above him. He closed his eyes. The pillar of light remained as an after image. The lighting moved and he opened his eyes.

"The garden shears! Esmé!" He was screaming over the deafening roar of electricity. Then, as quickly as the electricity had turned on them, it was gone. Silence fell over the room. The ritual had failed. The requirements had not been met. Esmé was no virgin.

Esar-Haden opened his eyes. The ghostly after image was slow to fade but he was still able to map the room. Seruli was dead, heaped in a corner, his body smoldering. The elven wizard was alive, on all fours, his head down, trying to vomit but unable to. The succubus had been driven back to the cave's wall. She was half collapsed against the blasted stone, but still somehow kept her feet under her. Her once perfect skin was criss-crossed with wounds which seeped black blood. She touched her lower abdomen, in the gap between her corset and her skirt. A deep gash revealed the tender meat within. Esar-Haden returned his gaze to Esmé.

"Esmé. I need you."

Esmé registered his voice. She halted her efforts to calm the pain and turned her head a degree. She offered her profile to him but she was not entire conscious of her actions. She was in a daze.

"The shears," he said. "Your gardening shears."

She turned her head still further. She twisted her torso. "Esar?"

"Esmé—the shears! You must have tucked them into your belt. Do you remember? Cut me free."

Esmé reached down and grabbed the shears. The tang of burnt flesh filled the air. She rolled over, now facing Esar-Haden.

Esar-Haden turned onto his side. He twisted his neck, looking over his shoulder at Esmé. "Cut the rope."

Esmé cut the rope. Esar-Haden worked his hands free. He took the shears from her, they were cooling but still painful to hold. He reached down, and cut his feet free of their bindings.

"Finally," he cursed, tossing the shears aside.

Esar-Haden got to his feet, crouching next to Esmé. "Can you walk?"

She only moaned in response.

Esar-Haden scanned the cave. "There you are." He left Esmé's side and rushed over his belt. The sole remaining dagger had fallen out of its sheath. He picked up his belt, scooped up his dagger, and dropped it into one of the empty sheaths. He returned to Esmé and thrust an arm under hers. He began to lift her up. "Come on."

Despite all she had endured Esmé found her feet. She clung to him. Esar-Haden half carried her, half pushed her toward the hall. As he approached the exit of the cave a figure stumbled into view. It was Esmé's brother. He held a slender wand in his hand. His other arm hung limp at his side. The elven wizard started to speak, perhaps to activate the wand, perhaps to threaten Esar-Haden, either way, he never got the words out.

Esar-Haden flung Esmé forward. She collided into her brother, knocking the wand wide. Her brother twisted his body, causing her to ricochet off of him. She collapsed in a heap next to him with a pained yelp. The elven wizard looked to Esar-Haden. He was surprised to see the dark elf was face-to-face with him. He started to bring the wand up, but it was too late.

He became aware of a sharp pain in his abdomen. He glanced down and saw a dagger buried in his stomach. The wand slipped from his fingers. Esar-Haden let go of the dagger's handle and stepped back. The wizard fingered the pommel. Esar-Haden reached forward and withdrew his second dagger from the elven wizard's belt. "No souvenir for you," he said, as he replaced the blade in its sheath. The elven wizard started to stumble backwards but Esar reached out and steadied him.

The elven wizard searched the room, tilting his head to see past Esar-Haden.

"There," said Esar-Haden, leaning to the side so that the elven wizard could see the succubus. She sat against the wall, her stocking legs sticking straight out. A pool of black blood radiated out from her.

"She's dying," observed Esar-Haden.

The elven wizard looked into his face. The news seemed to shock him.

"I tried to warn you," said Esar-Haden. Esmé staggered to her feet. "Sorry about that, darling. I had to think fast." She was studying her brother's back. A look of realization then horror crossed her face. Esar-Haden frowned. He knocked the elf's hand away and took ahold of the dagger's hilt. He slid the knife out. In his periphery he saw Esmé flutter to the floor like a leaf.

"My mistress is—dying?" The elven wizard reached out and grabbed Esar-Haden's arm to steady himself. His legs were growing weak.

"You're dying."

The elven wizard once again looked at him with a shocked expression. The color drained from his face and he wobbled. He reached out with his other hand, somehow getting his injured arm to respond. Esar-Haden offered his other arm and the wizard took it.

A trickle of blood found its way between his lips and dribbled from his chin. "When did you?"

"You left us together all day."

"I never—"

"The seduction route—" began Esar-Haden.

"But—"

"I told you it was double-edged."

The elven wizard glanced down at Esmé then looked back at Esar-Haden. "It was a cute plan."

"You should have been a dark elf," said Esar-Haden.

"Maybe our souls will meet in the Abyss—cousin."

Esar-Haden shrugged his shoulders. The stomach wound sapped the wizard's remaining strength. He collapsed into a seated position. Esar-Haden knelt down with him. The wizard slid his hand down until it grasped Esar-Haden's. He studied his own pale skin as it contrasted against the ebony skin of his distant, darkness-dwelling cousin. He looked into Esar-Haden's eyes.

Esar-Haden watched as the elf's eyes glazed over. He lost his grip and settled down into dying. Esar-Haden stood and went to Esmé. He knelt and picked her up. He flung her over his left shoulder, keeping his right hand free incase he needed the dagger, not that he felt he would survive yet another "obstacle." He started out of the cave.

"Esar?"

Esar-Haden stopped and half turned, looking down at the slouched wizard. The dying elf began to cough. A line of blood and saliva hung from his mouth.

"You have a long walk home." He turned his head and looked up into Esar-Haden's eyes. "Sorry about that."

Esar-Haden turned and looked over his shoulder at the succubus. She was slumped forward, enduring her last moments of life. The elf looked to her as well. Esar-Haden looked down at Esmé's brother. "It will take some time to bleed out. You've got time to think." He turned and took a step into the hallway, then stopped, turning back. "Sorry about that."

The Killing Stroke

Being superior to others is nothing other than having people talk about your affairs and listening to their opinions. The general run of people settle for their own opinions and thus never excel. Having a discussion with a person is one step in excelling him. A certain person discussed with me the written materials at the clan office. He is better than someone like me in writing and researching. In seeking correction from others, you excel them.

- Hagakure,
Yamamoto Tsunetomo

"One often hears it said that life means less to a dark elf than to any other race."

Esar-Haden set down the ceramic cup and at the same time dropped his other hand below the table. He slid one of his twin daggers from its sheath and held it in his lap. The hot wine sent up a pillar of steam between him and the unknown speaker. The speaker approached without a sound. That troubled the ever alert rogue, especially given how sensitive his hearing was. He looked through the steam into the face of an elderly man.

The man stood erect. There was still much physical vigor in him, defying the expected infirmity of his years, but it was fading. Esar-Haden noticed that the man's hips were at a slight angle, his knees loose. This told him that the man's feet were set in a well balanced stance. The unexpected visitor wore only a simple open-front shirt and long, wide-legged pants. His tan chest was bare, hidden only by a fine coat of wiry, white hair. There was a curved blade in a scabbard at his hip. He had one hand on the hilt. His forearms were criss-crossed with scars.

Esar-Haden took this in with a glance. He also understood that even though he had a dagger free and the man's blade was sheathed, he was seated and the man had position. To act was to invite death. "Appearances are not what they seem," he mumbled, as he brought his hand above the table and set his blade down next to the cup of hot wine.

The man smiled. He moved his hand from the hilt of his sword. "May I share a drink with you?"

Esar-Haden indicated the empty bench.

"Why didn't you act?" enquired the man. "Your blade was free and I am old, hardly a threat."

"You know why."

The man nodded. A woman approached the table with a ceramic jug of wine. She set a cup before the old man. She looked into his face as she poured the steaming wine and recognized him. Her eyes grew wide. Her eyebrows rose in alarm and she hurried back to the kitchen, pulling her long skirt up with one hand, her slippered feet half-running, half-scooting.

"There is a time to act," said the man, "and a time not to act. Understanding this truth can often mean the difference between life and death."

"Both are true," said Esar-Haden.

The man nodded, thinking the dark elf had agreed with his truism, which he had. He then realized Esar-Haden had said "both." He smiled, understanding that his initial statement had been verified as well. 'Will he live up to the reputation of his race? Does life mean less to them that to all others?' The man asked himself. "You are known among the Baì."

"I've done work for them," said Esar-Haden.

"They're little more than highwaymen and street thugs."

Esar-Haden nodded. He reached to his cup and lifted it to his lips. When he set the cup down he slid his hand over to his dagger. The man watched. Esar-Haden dragged the blade across the table, lowered it out of the old man's view, and slid it back into its sheath.

"Assassin's work?" asked the man.

Esar-Haden shook his head.

"They've not asked?"

"Not allowed."

The man raised an eyebrow.

Esar-Haden downed the rest of the wine and banged his fist on the table. He glanced to the kitchen door to see if the woman was returning. He saw a man standing in the doorway, looking at their table. The woman peered from around his shoulder. Esar-Haden held up the cup. The man in the doorway spun, nearly knocking the girl over. The door shut as he disappeared into the kitchen. Esar-Haden looked back to the old man seated across from him. "Something about assassinations being out of their purview," he said. "I'm guessing some other powerful group has claimed that work."

"Perhaps," said the old man. "Would you, though? Do such work?"

"Depends—" began Esar, but he was cut off.

The door to the kitchen opened and the same woman as before came out. She carried a small rectangular tray. She hurried to the table and bowed to the old man.

"Please forgive me, Master," she said. "I am a stupid female. My slow mind did not immediately recognize you. A hundred apologies." She motioned to the tray without rising from her bent posture. "My father has made these for you and your companion. I have also brought our best wine. Please accept these offerings along with our apologies. Our humble establishment is unfit for your presence. May I pour your wine, Master?"

The man was momentarily embarrassed but recovered. "Please, rise. It is inappropriate for you to bow to me in your father's house." He looked to the woman. She did not rise but remained bent at the waist, looking to the floor. The man looked to the tray. "Yes, wine for myself and my companion."

The woman rose, picked up the ceramic jug, and poured the steaming wine with great care. She set the plate of delicacies between the two men and set two pairs of chopsticks on the rim of the plate. She then reversed course and, bent the entire time, made her way backwards through the kitchen door.

The old man turned back to Esar-Haden. "Well," he said with a frown. "I thought these peasant's clothes would disguise me."

"I still don't know who you are."

This made the old man smile.

"You, I planned to tell. It was these commoners," the man glanced around the room, "who spread gossip quicker than a dry field spreads fire," he looked back to Esar-Haden, "whom I wished to deceive." The man waved his hand. "Eh? What can one do? Gossip is gossip, one can ignore it or repeat it, one cannot stop it."

This made Esar-Haden smile. He reached out and picked up his cup, eager to taste the best wine of the establishment. "To gossip, then." The old man picked up his cup, raised it, and smiled. Both men drank. "What have you come to gossip about?"

The man picked up a pair of the chopsticks and looked over the delicacies. "Now that my presence is no doubt the topic of the house," he selected and picked up a round ball of fried dough, filled with fruit paste and covered with sesame seeds, "We'd best finish our wine and depart."

Esar-Haden picked up the other pair of chopsticks and looked from the old man to the plate. They ate and drank in silence. When the food was consumed and the jug emptied, the old man rose. He pulled a small pouch from his belt. From this he fished out a few silver coins. He tossed the coins on the table. Esar-Haden followed him outside into the evening twilight.

The old man turned and led them towards the edge of town. Shop keepers exited their stores to light the street lanterns. Both Esar-Haden and the old man watched to make sure they weren't followed. After both parties felt secure the old man spoke.

"My name is Vazzo." He looked to the dark elf. "A retainer to our Excellency."

"That surprises me," admitted Esar-Haden.

"Why?"

Esar-Haden pointed to the man's forearms, to the matting of scar tissue. "Nobles don't usually sport such a fine collection."

"You've a few?"

"In the off chance that my childhood hadn't provided me with ample scars," answered Esar-Haden, "my years at the military academy ensured that I reached my quota."

Vazzo laughed. "And thus you recognize the results of practice with a live blade."

Esar-Haden pulled up his sleeve to reveal similar scars. "I've not as many as your high and noble self," he said, smiling. "Perhaps I've been a quicker study than you," he added, winking to the old man.

Vazzo gave him a wry smile. "It is a pleasure to speak with one who does not always strive to kiss my behind." They walked a bit more in silence. A sombre mood overcame the old man. "There is good reason daughter and father behaved as they did. Indeed, they would have done anything I asked and were undoubtedly relieved when I left." He looked at Esar-Haden. "Not out of respect, mind you, out of fear. Long ago I founded a sword school called the School of Six Hundred Killing Strokes." He looked to Esar-Haden. "Ah, now you regard me differently."

"I've heard of your school," said Esar-Haden. "I was warned to stay away from your pupils."

Vazzo looked at him, then away. "You speak to the master."

"At least I drank some good wine before being sent to my maker."

Vazzo seemed not to register the gallows humor. "Myself and my pupils fulfill a much needed role in his Excellency's administration. It is to me he turns on the eve of battle, to ensure that victory follows. It is to me that he expresses his grievances, so that his wrath is felt. These things I am glad to do, for I have sworn my life to such endeavors." He looked to Esar-Haden. "I have built my school slowly, carefully, selecting only the most disciplined students. I cared not whose sons they were. I cared not how much gold was placed in my hand to buy admission —I tossed it away. I care only about devotion, loyalty, and discipline. My school grew in strength. We killed or absorbed our rivals. In time we were feared. I offered my services to the Emperor. Long have I fulfilled this role. Now, in my old age, I find that nothing last forever."

The lights of the town were behind the pair. A bamboo grove lie ahead, covering a small hill. Rice paddies extended to either side. Evening birds expressed their pre-slumber wishes to one another. The road turned and made its way between the fields. With the sun gone, the half moon took command of the sky. Its light transformed the long, thin bamboo leaves into miniature sparkling blades.

The man turned to face the dark elf. "While peasants fear me, my own hold me more and more in contempt," he said. "The man I thought most loyal to me has maneuvered against me. He has almost convinced the Emperor that I am a tottering old fool whose strength has left him."

"I can't imagine that," said Esar-Haden.

"You might come to believe it as my tale unfolds," said Vazzo. He became lost in contemplation. The two studied the heavens until Vazzo spoke again. "When the alpha wolf weakens, his infirmity threatens the survival of the pack. In such a situation the pack attacks him. He knows this act comes and it is his final duty to fight them and to die with honor. In this way the pack remains strong. They do not conspire behind his back, weaken him, and finally tear his throat while he sleeps." The old man clenched his fist, his face twisted in disgust. His features soon softened and he lowered his arms and splayed his fingers. "I have no male heir, only daughters. Believe me, I tried to produce a son. I have taken four wives in my time." He looked to Esar-Haden. "I do not see a daughter as less than a son. I have seen the warrior spirit manifest in both men and women." He looked away, to the darkness at the heart of the bamboo grove. "Still, I know that my pupils will not follow a woman, nor will the Emperor turn to a woman on the eve of battle." Vazzo looked at Esar-Haden. "You smile?"

Esar-Haden raised his hand, waving away any perceived insult. "Women rule my culture," he explained. "It is the males who are said to be inferior. Where I come from no woman would follow a man or turn to him on the eve of battle."

Vazzo nodded his head. He looked to the moon.

"Without a male heir my only choice was to pass my school down to my most promising student. I would marry my eldest daughter to this student. Their offspring, my grandchild, would, if born male, carry my blood and spirit and perhaps gain control of the school I've labored my entire life to establish. My school, all I have worked for, my legacy, would carry on past my death. An old man wants nothing more." Vazzo looked from the moon to the lights of the city. "I married my most dedicated pupil to my eldest. She is now pregnant with my grandchild. However, I find my wishes perverted. My pupil is not loyal, to me or my daughter. He has no respect for me, for my daughter, or for my legacy. Despite his years of tutelage under my watchful eye he has deceived me. He works to turn my pupils against me. He slanders me to the Emperor. He has subjugated my daughter to his cruel will. If he has his way he will destroy my legacy while I still live."

"Kill him." At saying this, Esar-Haden witnessed something come over the man. His shoulders slumped. He looked to the ground. "You don't think you can?"

Vazzo looked to Esar-Haden. "He is careful. He surrounds himself at all times with the best of my pupils. I poured all of my knowledge into him, treating him as my son. He is undoubtedly my equal, if not my better, for he has strength and vigor and I have old eyes and tired muscles." He looked away. "I am no longer young. I am half as fast as I once was. Age is a foe that cannot be defeated."

"You had the drop on me," observed Esar-Haden.

"Yes, I could have killed you." The man paused, then looked to the dark elf. "Might you not have also struck a killing blow?" He looked away. "I am not so certain of victory. If you had acted would I have been too slow?"

"You want me to kill your disciple?"

Vazzo looked once again to the dark elf. "You would never get close to him. It's impossible." He turned and looked to the bamboo trees. "I must choose now between my legacy and my revenge," stated Vazzo. "I fear the choice has been made for me. My legacy is lost. All that is left is my revenge." The old man paused. "He must understand my wrath. He must pay for his betrayal. I thought long and hard about how best to wound him. There seemed no way and I feared all was lost." He looked to Esar-Haden. "Finally, I understood how to strike him where he is unprotected." He lowered his head once again. "But I cannot bring myself to do it. Despite the vast number of men I have sent to their graves. Despite the fear those living have for my blade." He shook his head. The moonlight illuminated the tears running down his cheeks. "I *am* an old fool whose strength has left him." He brought his hands to his face.

"Where is he unprotected?" asked Esar-Haden. "Where could you strike?"

The old man wiped his eyes and regained his composure. He lifted his head and looked to the moon and stars. "My daughter." He looked to Esar-Haden. "I want you to kill my daughter and my unborn grandchild. If she is murdered he will lose the respect of those who now follow him. Even the Emperor will question his competence." He looked to the silver-coated leaves of the bamboo. "The greatest act of revenge is to destroy what one has created, so that he who covets it has nothing to steal."

Vazzo reached to his belt and untied his sword. He extended sword and scabbard to Esar-Haden. "This is the blade of Six Hundred Killing Strokes. I have built a school with this blade. I want you to tear it down with this blade."

It is good to carry some powdered rouge in one's sleeve. It may happen that when one is sobering up or waking from sleep, his complexion may be poor. At such a time it is good to take out and apply some powdered rouge.

- *Hagakure,*
  Yamamoto Tsunetomo

Act Two

His name was Cassell and Esar-Haden followed him and his entourage for several days. He learned their patterns and habits. As the old assassin had said, Cassell was always surrounded. There were times when Vazzo's daughter was not at his side, times in which Esar-Haden could have carried out his employer's wishes. Esar-Haden did not strike. He waited and watched.

Perhaps it was some sixth sense, or perhaps it was simply a mood that came over him, but now Cassell kept Vazzo's daughter by his side at all times. Her stomach was full with child, yet she was thin in limb. She was not entirely unattractive. She had something of the old man's eyes and his wide forehead. Other than these recognizable features she had a round face, puffy cheeks, and a small mouth. She had straight, black hair cut just below the ears. She was unsteady on her thin legs, still, Cassell pulled her impatiently behind him by her wrist.

The pair, surrounded by six young, fierce-looking swordsmen from the school, passed Esar-Haden while walking up the plank ramp leading to the ferry. Several youths eyed the dark elf. He smiled and nodded to each, only to receive a sneer in reply. Esar-Haden mounting the ramp last. He glanced to the spot in the tall reeds where he had hidden his twin daggers and the old man's katana. By way of defense he had only the spells native to his people, the half-remembered spells taught to him by his former lover, Soléne, and the hand-to-hand techniques taught to him at the military academy in Pwyll. Most importantly, though, he had his wits.

Three men with long poles pushed the boat from the shore. It began its way down the river. A cold drizzle began and the passengers went below deck. They sat on mats, commoner and noble alike. There was little else in the low-ceilinged space. There were no windows. Blades of light came from between the boards above. The space was further illuminated by lanterns, the smoke finding its way out through gaps. The lanterns, which were suspended from the ceiling, swayed gently as the boat was pushed along.

A child made his way among the passengers offering rice balls and warm wine at an "affordable price." When he made a sale he rushed back to his mother to hand her the money. He did not offer one to the strange man with ebony skin, pointed ears, violet eyes, and white hair.

Cassell sat cross-legged in the center of the room, surrounded by his followers, holding his wife close to his side. He occasionally glanced at the dark elf passenger. He had never seen a dark elf. None of the passengers had. His bodyguards studied all of the ferry's occupants. They found none as threatening as Esar-Haden.

During his days of observation, Esar-Haden had seen the group take the ferry down river to a large plantation. They were accompanied by the peasants who worked the plantation's rice fields. A little outpost had grown up on the shore next to the plantation where the ferry stopped and the workers disembarked. This included a small drinking and gambling establishment. Esar-Haden was not sure what business Cassell had with the plantation's owner. Perhaps he was a relation. Or perhaps Cassell was strengthening some political tie with the rich owners. It mattered not. It didn't figure into the plan.

Cassell leaned over and spoke to one of the young men. Both Cassell and the youth were looking at Esar-Haden. The youth rose. He had to bend somewhat to avoid hitting his head on the room's low ceiling. He approached Esar-Haden, hand on the hilt of his sword. Esar-Haden felt an instinctual impulse to reach for his own daggers. He had to remind himself that his daggers, and Vazzo's sword, were well out of reach. The young man sat on his heels, knees together, in front of Esar-Haden. His hand was still on his sword.

"Who are you?"

"No one," said Esar-Haden.

"You have no name?"

"My name is Viati," lied Esar-Haden.

"What are you doing on this ferry?"

Esar-Haden chuckled. The youth frowned and tightened his grip on his sword. Esar-Haden held out his hands, palms up. "Looking for a game of skill or chance. Cards, dice, whatever comes. You play?"

"A gambler?"

"That's right," said Esar-Haden, nodding. "I like to test my luck. It thrills me." Esar-Haden lifted his chin to reveal the large black letters inked on his throat. He doubted the youth would be able to see much of them in the poor light of the below-deck room. Even if he could see the tattoo, Esar-Haden knew he would not know that it said, "Thrilled," in the dark elf language.

The youth glanced at the tattoo and then looked back into Esar-Haden's face. "Where do you come from?"

"Far to the west."

"Why have you come here?"

"I owe money everywhere else." Esar-Haden smiled. "What do you say to a game of dice? I have some on me. I'll teach you a game from my homeland."

Esar-Haden reached into his jacket. The youth's hand shot out to grab his wrist. Esar-Haden saw that another of Cassell's entourage stood and started over. The youth pulled Esar-Haden's hand free. He looked down at the pair of ivory dice held in the dark elf's long, thin fingers. The youth flung Esar-Haden's arm to the side. He kept his eyes locked onto Esar-Haden's as he reached in and searched the folds of his jacket. Finding nothing he pulled his hand back. The second youth circled around the pair and sat at Esar-Haden's back. Esar-Haden looked over his shoulder. "Sit here, eh?" He pointed to a spot in front and to the side. "I know a game for three players. You've got coin?" He looked back and forth between the youths. The first youth looked over his shoulder at Cassell, who had been listening to the entire exchange. Cassell studied Esar-Haden. The look in his eyes was one of dismissal. He looked to his wife. The youths rose and made their way back to their master.

Esar-Haden tossed the dice in the air, caught them, and stuffed them back into his interior jacket pocket. "Hey, boy," he called to the child-merchant. "I need a drink—for luck. I've got coin that's as good as anyone else's." He waved to the child. As the child cautiously approached, Esar-Haden glanced at Cassell and his men. They were no longer concerned with him and spoke amongst themselves. "Good, good," said Esar-Haden to the boy. He thought, however, of the old man's truism. This had been the time *not* to act.

. . .

Two days later Esar-Haden sat cross-legged on a pillow at the corner of a large rectangular table. A bundle containing everything he needed for the job was tucked under his legs. The table was cut away in the middle. The space was piled high with pillows. On these sat a woman in a long silk dress. She played a stringed instrument that rested in her lap. Esar-Haden had never seen such an instrument. It was something like a lute and a harp mixed together and it sounded wonderful played with such skill, as it was. The woman's back was to him. Instead of an unknown man, a dark elf no less, she chose to face a rich nobleman, one who often spent great sums on wine and women. A woman with a painted face knelt next to the nobleman, her hand in his lap.

The two men were the exclusive establishment's only patrons. The night was young, however. It had cost Esar-Haden a small fortune to bribe the host to allow him entry. He was lucky indeed to have cleaned out the gambling room down river two days prior, otherwise he would have had to come up with a different plan.

Even though he had gained entry he was treated differently than the nobleman. None of the women with painted faces came near him. The waiter had been reluctant to bring him wine or food. Finally, Esar-Haden pulled out his coin purse and stacked his silver and gold coins on the table in front of him. This brought the waiter. The painted women eyed the stack, debating.

Esar-Haden waited. He drank little wine and only nibbled at his food. He listened to the music and offered the musician some coins. She demurely accepted. In time one of the more brave, or, perhaps greedy, geisha approached. She knelt next to him and bowed her head. Esar-Haden began to coax her into conversation. He slipped coin after coin into her small, delicate hands. Soon she was talking freely, drinking the wine he bought her, and even seemed to be having a good time.

This was the scene that Cassell, his captive wife, and his six bodyguards saw when they entered the restaurant and brothel. Esar-Haden had been expecting them, although he seemed to pay them no heed. His attention, to all observers, was on the young painted woman with whom he laughed and flirted. Cassell dispatched the same two youths as before. They approached Esar-Haden from opposite sides.

"What are you doing here?" asked the same young man who had interrogated him before.

Esar-Haden halted his laughter and looked up at the young man. "Ah. You again." He laughed. "You must be good luck. Look!" Esar-Haden swung his hand out to indicate the stacks of coins. He knocked them over, feigning intoxication. The coins scattered across the table and tumbled onto the pillows. "Oops," he said to the woman, both laughing.

"I'll get them for you." She giggled. She climbed onto the table and reached into the pile of pillows, retrieving the coins. Esar-Haden reached up and patted her on the rump. He looked up to the youths.

"You're still here?" he asked, laughing. "You must want to try your luck. Eh? Dice or cards? You have coin, don't you? I'm spending mine too quickly!" Esar-Haden glanced across the room at Cassell, who was arguing with the establishment's host. The host was pointing to the coins that the young geisha was carefully stacking. She was, of course, tucking many away in the pockets and folds of her dress. Growing frustrated, Cassell waved the man away. He called to the two youths, who returned to him.

As the evening progressed the room filled with patrons. Wine flowed. Sumptuous dishes were passed around the table. The laughter and pleasurable cries of the women were heard above the music. Esar-Haden was running dangerously short of funds. His many stacks had diminished to a few lonely coins. However, the woman at his side was drunk and happy. He waved over to the host who approached.

"I must bed this woman!"

"Please, please," said the host, looking around the room at the other patrons. "This is not that kind of establishment." He bent and whispered to Esar-Haden. "This way. Follow." The host assisted Esar-Haden to his feet, reaching out to sweep the dark elf's remaining coins into his own pocket. "Come, come." Encouraged the host, leading Esar-Haden and the drunken geisha out of the room.

. . .

The woman pulled herself out of her dress, almost falling as she did so. She clung to Esar-Haden, kissed him, pulled his face into her breasts, commanded, "Suck!" then collapsed onto the bed and fell asleep. Esar-Haden admired the smallness of her frame and the rise of her butt that reflected the moonlight shining through the open window. He reached out and patted her bare behind.

'Not tonight,' he thought.

He folded the blanket over the woman. He set his bundle down and unwrapped it. He stripped naked and began to apply rouge to his arms, neck and upper chest, the back of his hands and finally to his face and neck. He produced a small metal mirror from his pack and angled it in the moonlight. 'Well, you don't quite have the color of the old man, but it will fool their wine-addled minds.'

He put the container of rouge away. He set the sword aside and dressed in simple peasant clothing, similar to those that the old man had used as a disguise. He pulled a pair of shears from the pack and cut his hair to the necessary length, letting his white strands fall onto the spread cloth. He put the shears away and picked up the sword and scabbard. He drew Vazzo's sword partially free. 'A hell of a blade,' he thought, holding the Six Hundred Killing Strokes sword to the shaft of moonlight.

He found the water basin and wet a towel. He left this in the basin, setting a dry towel next to it. He set his own clothes on the bed next to the sleeping woman. He hooked his belt and daggers on the bed post. If he had to leave in a hurry he could grab them and flee. He went to the door, opened it a crack, and looked out into the hall. He looked back into the room, looking over his preparations. He noticed a chair in the corner, and went to it. He pulled it next to the door and peered back into the hall. Seeing no one he exited the room, shutting the door behind him.

He listened at the other doors in the hallway and found that "it's not that kind of establishment" was doing good business, judging from the moans of pleasure he heard. Several doors were unlocked. He cautiously but quickly explored the empty rooms. He found the one he was searching for. It was a guess, but likely choice. It was the only suite composed of two rooms, a foyer and a bedroom. If Cassell was going to indulge his passions and retain the use of his bodyguards, this would be the room. He stepped into the room and shut the door behind him.

He went to the bedroom and looked around. The room was lit only by the moonlight coming through the open window. There was a lantern on the small table. He went to it and took out the wick, tucking it into his pocket. He looked up and smiled. 'My good fortune continues,' he thought. He climbed up onto the bed, jumped up and grabbed one of the criss-crossed ceiling beams, hauled himself up, crouched, and waited.

. . .

The muscles of his calves and thighs had been screaming in agony for some time when the door to the bedroom opened and one of the youths in Cassell's entourage stepped into the room. He glanced around then stepped to the side. Cassell entered the room, dragging his wife behind him. A second woman hurried through the door before the youth exited, shutting the door behind him.

Cassell tossed his wife onto the bed. He turned as the second woman threw herself at him, kissing him, clawing at his clothes. The two, Cassell and the painted whore, began to unclothe one another. Vazzo's eldest daughter scooted up to the corner of the bed where she lie on her side, curled into a ball, holding her baby-swollen stomach with one hand, covering her face with the other, in an attempt to hide her weeping.

Cassell worked with greater effect than the prostitute. He stripped her bare while he himself stood in his pants, bare chested. He spun her around him, then pushed her onto the bed. She looked up at him. Esar-Haden felt his nerves alight. 'She's going to see me,' he thought. He began to move his hand to the hilt of the sword. He stopped when the woman looked down to Cassell's belt string.

Cassell bent and reached over the naked woman. He grabbed his wife's ankle and pulled on it. "What are you doing? Crying?" He laughed. "We've got a lively one tonight." He snorted as she pulled her ankle free of his grasp. He waved her away, returning his attention to the prostitute.

"Have I had you before?" he asked.

She shook her head, rose up to her knees, threw her arms around him and began to kiss and caress him.

Esar-Haden watched and waited.

"What do you think, wife? You could learn from her. Such passionate kisses!" He laughed. Vazzo's daughter stifled her cries. Cassell spoke to the geisha. "She's no fun, is she?"

The geisha looked at the weeping woman curled on the bed. "Does she always cry?"

"A spoiled brat. She will learn her place. Forget her," said Cassell, "now is the time for *our* pleasure to begin," he announced. "Don't look away," he said to his wife. "You must learn to behave like her." He laughed, tugging on his wife's arm. She did not turn, as he wished. She scooted as far to the edge of the bed as she could get without falling. Her swollen belly hung precariously out over the void. She held it with both hands.

Cassell and the geisha resumed their passionate kissing and caressing. Vazzo's daughter cried too loudly for her husband's patience. He bent forward and grabbed a handful of her hair. He wrenched her head to the side so he could see her face. He let go of her hair and backhanded her. Given the awkward positioning of his body the blow was not hard but it had gotten his point across. She returned to her fetal posture.

"Always complaining," he growled. He returned his attention to the paid-for-woman.

Esar-Haden unsheathed the sword. He held it pointed downwards, dipping it into the shaft of moonlight entering through the window. He angled the sword, picking up the light, reflecting onto the weeping woman's cheek. Her face was turned away and she did not notice.

As Cassell and the geisha lost themselves in passion, Esar-Haden continued to pass the shaft of reflected light over Vazzo's daughter's face, the pillow she rest her head on, and the blanket at the edge of the bed. She noticed and lifted her head to follow the unexpected movement of light.

She turned her head and sought out its source. Esar-Haden lifted the blade out of the moonlight. Vazzo's daughter searched the rafters. Her eyes finally saw the presence crouched in the darkness. Esar-Haden held a finger to his lips. He hoped that she wasn't so brainwashed as to alert her husband or worse, to call out to the swordsmen in the adjoining room.

She squinted into the darkness above her. "Father?" she mouthed.

Esar-Haden nodded his head. He lowered the sword back into the moonlight. She looked at it, recognizing it. She looked to the couple next to her in the bed. She knew her father, knew his life's work, and suspected his present purpose. She slid herself from the bed, backed up, and stood next to the window with her back to the wall. The moonlight illuminated half of her face as she looked into the rafters.

The geisha was either genuinely enjoying Cassell's attention or was putting on a fine act. She was making all the right noises at his touch. He was drawn in by her responses and had all but forgotten his wife's presence in the room.

Vazzo's daughter reached up and wiped the tears from her face. She looked to her husband and the woman he touched. She looked back to the man she mistook for her father crouching in the darkness in the rafters above. Esar-Haden motioned that she should step to the side, in front of the window. He wanted her to block as much of the feeble light as she could. Darkness was an important part of his plan.

'Any second now,' thought Esar-Haden, as he monitored Cassell's actions. He gripped the sword with both hands, balancing on the narrow beam. The geisha assisted him without knowing.

"I'm ready for you," she whispered into Cassell's ear. "I need to feel you."

"Yes, yes," said Cassell between kisses. "You cannot resist me, can you?"

"Please, hurry, I ache for you," moaned the geisha.

"See, wife," said Cassell, "this is how a real woman responds to a man's touch." He glanced at the spot where he believed his wife was curled up, weeping. He was momentarily puzzled to see only the crumpled sheet.

Esar-Haden dropped from the rafters. He landed next to the bed, driving the tip of the sword of Six Hundred Killing Strokes into Cassell's unprotected back. The sword pierced Cassell's torso, split his romance-quickened heart, exited his body, and just nicked the geisha.

Both Cassell and the woman screamed. Esar-Haden reached and covered the geisha's mouth. She looked at him, her eyes wide, then fainted, falling backwards onto the bed, Cassell's body falling on top of hers, the sword sliding free. A jet of blood shot from the wound.

Esar-Haden looked to the door. Long moments passed. The door remained closed. His sensitive ears picked up the chuckling and commentary of the youths. They had attributed the screams to something more pleasurable than dying. They took the silence in the room for two spent people, and in a way they were right.

Esar-Haden angled his head, letting his hair fall over his face. He didn't want Vazzo's daughter getting a good look at him. He felt the warmth of the blood as it washed over him. 'Perfect,' he thought. He knew that the blood would only add to the effect he hoped to have in a moment.

Cassell was dead. The geisha had fainted, or was smart enough to pretend. Either way, she wasn't a problem for the moment. That was good, he didn't want to kill her. The job wasn't over, though. Cassell's bodyguards must be dealt with. They were a necessary part of the plan, even if it required grim work to make use of them.

Esar-Haden grabbed Cassell's shoulder and slid him over the geisha, the blood providing ample lubrication, until his head hung over the edge of the bed. Esar paused for a moment then with a downward chop he cut off Cassell's head.

He bent and picked it up, turned, and went to the door. He paused and looked to Vazzo's daughter. She was staring at her husband's decapitated, blood-splattered corpse. Esar-Haden grunted and she looked to him. He motioned with his head that she should move to the safety of the corner. She obeyed.

The moonlight illuminated the grisly scene. Cassell's wound had sprayed blood on the walls. It ran down in rivulets. His blood dripped from the rafters. The mattress was a sponge now full of blood. Excess blood pooled on its surface, ran over the edges, and dripped onto the floor. The geisha could barely be seen. What could be seen of her, her bare legs and one arm, were motionless and splattered with blood. She looked just as much a corpse as her would-be lover.

Esar-Haden turned back to the door. He reached out and knocked the butt of the hilt against the wood. The conversation in the adjoining room died down. He took a step back and to the side. He wanted the full extent of the carnage to be seen and understood. He heard the swordsmen draw their blades and gather at the door. There was a soft knock then the door opened a few inches.

"Master?" The lead youth called into the darkness of the room.

"The true master is here," growled Esar-Haden. He did his best to mimic the old man's voice.

The door opened. Esar could see one of Vazzo's treacherous pupils standing in the doorway, sword drawn. He could see the rest of the youths gathered behind him. The swordsmen peered into the room. As their eyes adjusted, they began to grasp what they saw. Looks of horror crossed their faces. Their eyes went from the bed, with its blood and bodies, to Esar-Haden, who they mistook for Vazzo. Esar-Haden lifted Cassell's decapitated head. The students looked into the vacant eyes. The eternal scream of death lingered silently on Cassell's blood-filled mouth.

Esar-Haden threw the head at them and lunged forward, screaming with rage as he did so. To them he was a wild-haired, blood-soaked spirit of vengeance. The legendary and feared sword of Six Hundred Killing

154

Strokes jumped out of the moonlight, a flash of steel and blood. This was enough for them. Cassell's head bounced off of the chest of the lead student. Discipline and courage fled from the group. They followed it with haste.

Esar-Haden did not follow. Instead, he knelt next to Cassell's head. He righted it, held it in place, and drove the sword down into, and through, it. The blade bit into the wood of the floor. Esar-Haden lifted the head up the length of the blade until it rested against the tsuba, the hand guard. He stood erect. He heard Vazzo's daughter step from the corner of the room.

"Father," she whispered, "You—" Esar-Haden looked over his shoulder. She was looking down at Cassell's body. "—killed." She looked to Esar-Haden, thinking he was her father.

He looked away from her. He paused for effect, then, with a growl, said, "My legacy grows within you, not his." With this he walked from the room.

He crossed the second room, exited, turned, and walked down the hall. One of the other doors opened and a man and woman, both holding their robes closed to hide their nakedness, peered out. They watched as the blood-soaked man passed. They shut the door before he could turn his murderous attention to them.

Esar-Haden looked around. All of the other doors were closed. The hall was empty, although he heard activity at the base of the stairs. He opened the door to his own room and stepped in. He knew he didn't have much time. Eventually, someone would notice that the trail of blood stopped at his door.

He jammed the chair beneath the door handle. He stripped as he crossed the room, going to the basin. He tossed the bloody clothes onto the cloth square lying on the floor. He grabbed the wet towel and began to wash himself. He heard men cautiously mounting the stairs.

They stopped at the first door, knocked, and whispered, albeit loudly, to the occupants, commanding them to leave. Esar-Haden wrung out the wet towel in the basin. He tossed it on top of the bloody clothing. He grabbed the other towel and began to dry himself, scrubbing off the last of the rouge and blood.

There was a knock at the door.

"Eh? What?" Esar-Haden called out, mimicking a sleepy voice. He looked to the slumbering woman. She did not stir.

"You must leave immediately," came a nervous voice. The knock came again. Esar-Haden could hear other men passing by his door, moving cautiously.

"Okay, okay!" called Esar-Haden. He heard the man move away from his door. He went to the bed and dressed. He rolled up the cloth and tied it. He carried the basin to the window, glanced out, and dumped the bloody water into the street below. He grabbed his belt and daggers and put them on. He tied up his hair, grabbed his bag and the roll of cloth, and went to the window. He checked the street once more. Not seeing anyone he climbed out of the window and dropped down into the street. He walked along the edge of the building, turned the corner, and stepped into an alley.

Among the words spoken by great generals, there are some that are said offhandedly. One should not receive these words in the same manner, however.

> - *Hagakure,*
> Yamamoto Tsunetomo

"You did not do as I asked."

Esar-Haden set down the steaming cup of wine. He looked up and once again saw the old man staring down at him. Vazzo had no need for disguises and wore a white, crisply folded robe with elaborate embroidery. Esar-Haden followed Vazzo's bent arm to his sun-tanned and scared hand, which, gripped the hilt of the sword of Six Hundred Killing Strokes.

"Glad to see that found its way back to its proper owner," said Esar-Haden. He looked into Vazzo's wrinkled face. The old man's emotions were hard to gauge.

"You did not do as I asked," repeated Vazzo. He tightened his grip on the hilt of his sword. He need not shift his footing, as it was already in place. The door to the kitchen opened and the woman appeared. She saw the master of the School of Six Hundred Killing Strokes, spun, and disappeared into the kitchen.

Esar-Haden searched Vazzo's eyes. He sat upright, shoulders squared. He set his hands palms down on the table. "I did the thing you would have done, had you not already admitted defeat."

A tense moment passed. Vazzo did not move, nor did Esar-Haden. Esar-Haden did not look from the old man's face to his sword, even though he feared it. The steam from the wine rose between them. A smile crept across the old man's face. His hand fell from his sword to his side. "So the master becomes a student again."

He reached into his robe and produced a leather pouch. He tossed it on the table. Esar-Haden glanced at it and then looked back to Vazzo. The old man turned and walked to the door. He stopped and half-turned. "She feels that it's a boy," he announced, smiling. "She tells me the baby swings his arms about like a wild man."

"A swordsman," countered Esar-Haden.

Vazzo looked at him. He nodded, smiled, then stepped from the common room into the evening twilight.

Prince of Flies

Prince Lewin lay on his side, pained from a fall from the saddle. What had knocked him down he did not know.

Wind howled through the stones and lashed his body, causing him to curl himself in defense against its bite. He was not dressed for cold and even though he wore armor it retained in none of his body's warmth. He felt what he thought was sand strike his face, for he had been in the desert. However, the wind was bitterly cold and the "sand" was wet on his flesh. The wind turned. He tried to open his eyes but could not. He reached up and scraped the ice free from his face. He opened his eyes only to close them as the wind shifted back. It stayed but a moment before again changing direction. He sat up, shielded himself with an upraised hand, and looked.

Before him was the entrance to Pwyll, but not as he had last seen it. The defensive earthworks built by the dark elves were hidden by a frozen cascade of water, the origin of which he could not divine. He looked around. The hard-packed desert floor was covered with shimmering ice. Tendrils of snow shot in whichever direction the capricious wind desired.

Near him, the iron-shod hooves and long, bony-kneed legs of a horse rose, hooves high, from the ice. He was surrounded by horses, locked in various poses by ice and death. His own horse was close. He saw its head in profile: black lips curled, tongue hanging over blocky yellow teeth, flared nostrils frosted, mane glued by frozen blood, and a thin ledge of snow building on the curved surface of its glossy black eyes.

Prince Lewin struggled to his feet. He checked himself for injury and while sore he saw no wounds, felt no broken bones. He held his palm against the wind and looked around. Littered amongst the horses were dead dark elves. They, too, had been claimed by the ice. Their black armor resembled the backs of beetles caught in a sudden snow. Their white hair was lost in that other white. He saw wagons and siege works blackened by fire. The wind pulled ash from these carcasses, mingled it with the snow, and hid the sun with its swirling.

Opposite the ice-choked entrance, at the edge of the field of battle, Prince Lewin saw a dark elf female sitting cross-legged on the ice. She wore thick furs but her head, forearms, and hands were exposed. Her long white hair whipped like a flag of surrender. He squinted and studied her. A half-mask hid the upper part of her face and made it alien. He could see puffs of breath escape from her moving lips.

He pulled his sword free and approached. The dark elf woman was chanting a prayer. Now closer, he could make out the mask. It was black with a sparse coating of short, stiff, black hairs. The eyes were bulbous, shimmering, and multifaceted. The brilliance of the frozen scene was multiplied on the hundredfold surface of those eyes. The mask depicted a fly's face. He saw movement and looked to her forearms and hands. They were coated with congealed blood. Flies clung to her, their translucent wings bending in the wind. The swarm fed on the blood, sponging it, mopping it up with a thousand eager mouths.

'How do they survive the cold?'

The wind blew. The flies were not swept away.

'Or maintain their grip?'

Prince Lewin was about to speak when the wind pooled into a vortex about him, throwing up snow and ash, forcing him to close his eyes. The vortex was short-lived. When he opened his eyes the dark elf was gone. He saw movement where she had been. He thought it might be the flies, approached, knelt and examined them. It was not the flies, however, nor was the movement on the ice, but under it. He bent closer and saw with horror that there was a soldier under the ice who wore the colors of the Crown.

The soldier floated in a void. Only his face, shoulders, and uplifted arms could be seen. The rest of him was sunk in darkness. He had a wound on his forehead. Blood ran over the bridge of his nose, caught the slope of his cheek, fell, and vanished into the darkness. The soldier saw the prince and began to beat against the underside of the ice with his bloodied fists. He screamed for the prince's aid, his mouth twisting, but no sound reached Lewin's ears.

Prince Lewin dropped fully to his knees and beat the pommel of his sword against the ice. Flecks of ice launched into the air. The man trapped beneath the ice looked to his side. When he looked back his eyes were wide with fear. This contagious emotion spread to the prince, who slammed his pommel with all of his strength. With an ear-piercing crack the blade of his sword shattered into glittering shards. The handle split in his hand. The pommel shot off and disappeared in the snow.

He flinched away from the shattering of the blade. The metal bounced against the armor of his shoulder and arm and came to rest on the ice. He looked through the scattered shards, through the ice, into the soldier's face. The soldier looked to his side, then back to the prince. He beat his fists against the ceiling of ice. The soldier tried to maneuver away from whatever he saw, but there was nothing in the void from which to launch himself.

The soldier was grabbed by something Lewin could not see. He began to move. Lewin lost sight of him. He swept his arm out to the side, scattering the shards of metal, throwing the dusting of snow and ash into the air.

He caught a glimpse of the soldier. Lewin crawled after him, sweeping the snow, to keep sight of him. The man's unwanted movement sped up and Lewin regained his feet. He kept his eyes on the man and followed. The soldier looked up at the prince and screamed. He was yanked forward and was lost. Lewin stared unbelieving at the ice and the darkness beneath it.

The wind intensified, assaulting Prince Lewin. Mean-spirited cold found its way through every opening in steel and cloth, biting into his flesh. Lewin searched for cover. He saw the silhouettes of wind-carved red stones through the swirling snow and ash. He ran to the closest large stone and put his back to it. The wind reached him from around the corners. He searched for more effective shelter.

At the base of the next stone he saw the dark elf female. She was standing with her back to the stone, like him. Her furs hid all of her, even hooded her head. Only the ebony skin of her lower face and the bulging, multifaceted eyes of the mask could be seen. She waved for him to approach. He hesitated.

She pointed to a dark pool and yelled. Her voice was lost in the wind. She stepped away from the tower of stone, knelt—her form barely visible in the flurry of snow —and lowered herself into the darkness. Her head and shoulders reappeared. She waved for him, then dropped out of sight.

Prince Lewin knew he could not trust her. He knew she belonged to the enemy. He thought of the soldier under the ice, pulled along by some malevolent force or some unseen creature. He knew he had come to the edge of the desert and that even winter came here, but that did not make sense of this. The dark elf was the enemy, yes, but he realized that he would not last much longer in such harsh, supernatural weather.

He felt for the dagger at his hip, his sword gone, pulled it, and approached the dark pool. As he neared it he could discern that it was a natural opening in the rock. He lowered himself. He stood on a ledge of stone, his eyes adjusted to the feeble light. A dusting of snow settled on the ledge and the floor of the cave. He could not see much more than that. He climbed down, holding the dagger before him. The cave was quieter and calmer than the surface.

"Come," called a female voice from the darkness.

"I can't see."

He heard the striking of flint on stone and saw sparks fall. The head of a torch came alive with flame. The fire was lifted, held aloft. The cave and torchbearer came into view. The cave was small, shaped like an egg on its side, and featureless. The light of the torch disappeared into the mouth of a tunnel behind the dark elf woman. She reached up and pulled the hood down. She slid off the fly mask, revealing eyes that seemed to have been soaked in blood and had taken on that color.

"You need to warm yourself or you'll die," she stated. "Follow me." She turned and entered the tunnel.

Prince Lewin followed her. He wanted to ask her about the snow and ice. He wanted to ask her about the soldier he had seen, even about the strange mask she wore, yet caution held his tongue.

He began to suspect the dark elves had called upon powerful magics, had called on their dark gods, which were demons, if the rumors were true, which had sent the unnatural storm. The dark elf woman must have suspected his thoughts. She turned and looked over her shoulder.

"A strange fate grips you in its icy talons," she stated. Not expecting a response, she turned away from him and continued down the tunnel.

"We've been defeated," said Prince Lewin.

She laughed.

"We underestimated you."

"Obviously."

"Magic?"

She glanced over her shoulder but looked away without answering.

"We were assured that your people weren't disciplined enough to master the complexities of truly dangerous magic, magic of that sort," he glanced behind him, but could no longer see anything outside of the flickering pool of torchlight. "We were wrong."

"Not really," she replied. "Few dark elves manage a true mastery of magic. That sort of thing takes decades of quiet, undisturbed study." She spun. "Violence fills our lives and makes them chaotic and short." She studied him. "How old are you?"

He saw no reason to hide his age. "Sixteen."

"So young." She spun and continued to lead the way down the winding tunnel. The Prince's curiosity overcame him.

"Are we going to Pwyll?" he asked. "Will you ransom me?"

"Ransom?"

"We know your people will not survive the winter. You have no food stores. The citizens of Seven Rivers knew this as well. They feared an attack on their stores, so we came."

"Ah, the citizens of Seven Rivers." She sighed. "Unto them now is the moment of difficult choices."

"What will you do to them?"

"We are not a conquering people. We are a parasitic people," she said, in a matter-of-fact tone.

His concern returned to himself. He continued in the earlier vein. "The King, my father, will empty our granaries to get me back," he boasted with hopeful confidence.

She glanced over her shoulder at him, then looked away without speaking. They walked for a while.

"I saw something back there I did not understand," said Prince Lewin. "One of my father's men was under the ice. Come to think of it, I saw only horses and your own dead on the surface, none of my father's men. Perchance, were all of the King's men taken under the ice?" The thought caused him to shudder.

She paused. He stopped and looked at her, staring at the pool of darkness at the back of her head. The crackle of the fire echoed off of the stone.

"It's your own fate you should worry about." She turned her head so she could see him and he could see her face. "I can help you."

"What do you mean?"

She faced forward. "Where do you think you are?"

"In a tunnel, approaching Pwyll," he answered, looking at the stone walls and ceiling.

"You've already been to Pwyll," she said. "You were captured and taken to Maljamir. You were tossed at the feet of the demons. An offering of gratitude, not that they did a damn thing for us." She spun to face him. Her eyes traveled over him. "They began to fight over their prize; young, as you are, with noble features and pure blood. Oh, how they blazed with lust for you. How they wanted to use and hurt you." A wicked smile spread across her face. "Are you a virgin?" He did not answer. She stepped closer to him. He was tall for his age and looked down at her. "I plucked you from their grasp and threw you into Cocytus," she motioned with her head to the snow-blasted desert above. "Out of their reach."

"Cocytus?" He had never heard of such a land. He studied her. He could now see that her smooth ebony skin was marred by open wounds, spots where scabs had been picked free. As he looked at her he noticed a few flies crawl from wound to wound, feeding on her blood. The sores and the activity of the flies seemed not to irritate her. Her upraised arm held open her cloak. He saw no weapons. He held his dagger between them, emboldening him.

"A deception?" He returned his gaze to her sore-speckled face. "I've been warned against your treachery. There's no need to deceive me. I realize I'm a prisoner. As you said, I have royal blood. I would be better used for trade than for evil sport."

"What's a prince worth?" She chuckled. "In sacks of grain? Casks of ale? You think you'll be ransomed for bacon and bread?" As she spoke one of the flies launched itself from her cheek and buzzed close to his face. He reflexively lifted his free hand and waved it away. He watched as the fly circled back towards its host, spiraled on the updraft from the flame until it finally disappeared from the light. He returned his attention to his strange captor.

"If you're a parasite," he said, "feed."

The smile faded from her face. "You're quite sure of matters, for such a young man," she observed. "I can see you seated with the wisest men your father could compel to teach you. What did you learn from them? Eh? Theories of war? Of rulership? What good has it done you?" She waved her hand. "Here you are. Defeated and alone." She frowned. "That royal blood you boast of has filled you with false confidence."

She half turned and extended the torch. Prince Lewin could see that the tunnel opened into a cave. The ceiling disappeared into darkness. The light of the torch illuminated a rough pyramid of split logs between a pair of fur-lined sleeping pallets. He saw leather packs, various tools and supplies necessary for travel in a cold climate. There was something else, at the edge of light, that he couldn't quite make out. There was movement about it, and an unsettling smell.

The voice of the dark elf captured his attention. "Soon you'll be stripped of all illusions." She looked at him. "You face a truly horrible fate. But, I can save you." She entered the cave and lowered the torch to the split wood. "Just as I saved you from freezing to death."

The logs took the flames from the torch. The cave and tunnel mouth filled with light. She pulled the torch from the fire and held it close to her face, feeling its warmth. "And from," she paused. A sinister grin spread over her face. Her eyes rolled to the side, flashing evil at him, "whatever was under the ice."

The fire light crawled over the strange object at the edge of the camp, as did a multitude of flies. It dawned on Prince Lewin what the misshapen heap was. It was the sword-chopped remains of a fallen soldier. He caught glimpses of white flesh under the thick blanket of flies. Movement interrupted his view of the corpse. His hostess swung the torch violently, extinguishing it.

"What's your name?" asked Prince Lewin as the female dark elf stripped out of her clothing. She did not attempt to hide her nakedness. Just before modesty forced him to avert his gaze he caught a glimpse of the patches of raw, bloody flesh that covered an alarming portion of her body. She crawled into her pile of furs, holding their edges up, allowing flies, leaving their cold-corpse meal for her warm blood, to swarm her naked form. She enclosed herself and the flies in her furs without answering him.

For some time he heard her mumbling over the crackle of the fire and the buzzing of the flies. Her one-sided conversation was accompanied by giggles, moans, and movement under the fur. Eventually, she quieted. He could see the rhythmic rise and fall of her blankets.

He knew he should strip out of his wet clothing and heavy, ice-encrusted armor, and wrap himself in the furs. He did not feel safe enough. He sat on his pallet. He pulled the furs around his legs and waist. His companion was asleep, or seemed to be, and he was exhausted.

He knew he was missing time. He remembered the assault on Pwyll. General Ord had the men and horses working to dislodge the boulders the dark elves had packed into the cave opening, the opening that led to Pwyll. He remembered that the dark elves had attacked, a surprise attack, while the men were unprepared. It was chaos. He had been well away from the assault, just incase, yet he rushed forward, his retinue chasing him. All else seemed a blur and then he awoke in the snow and ice.

If the dark elf was telling the truth much had transpired that he was unaware of. He could not believe it, even though he had felt the cold and seen the soldier under the ice. The talk of demons fighting over him was ludicrous.

Yes, he had been taught by wise scribes and learned men, and yes, even these men said other planes existed whose inhabitants were monsters or worse, yet to think he had left one world and gone to another was simply too much to believe. He had nothing in his experience to match it.

He found his head nodding, eyelids drooping. As wary as he was of the bizarre dark elf, he could no longer stave off exhaustion. He stretched out on his side, pulled the furs on top of him, and closed his eyes.

. . .

"Prince Lewin!" a voice yelled. He opened his eyes and sat up. All was dark. He realized that he was not under the furs. Nor was he in his armor, for the weight and chill of it was absent. He felt around him. He was on a floor of stone, as before, but there was nothing padding his sleep nor covering him. He felt his person and discovered only rags.

"Prince Lewin!" called a man's voice. Lewin became aware of a rectangle of light hovering on the wall across from him. He stood and was now eye-level with the light. He felt around him in the darkness as he approached it. He discerned it was a small glassless window through which candle-light shone. He peered through and saw the face of a male dark elf.

"Prince Lewin, give me your hand," the dark elf commanded.

"What?" he asked, confused. "Where am I? What's happened?"

"Give me your hand."

"I was in a cave," protested Lewin. "There was a woman."

The candle was snuffed out. Darkness pressed in on all sides. "Wait! Wait, please."

The candle was re-lit. Prince Lewin saw the male dark elf.

"Give me your hand."

"What are you going to do?" asked Lewin.

"Place food in it."

At the mention of food Lewin's stomach began to ache. He hesitantly reached through the window. The dark elf male set the candle down. The light of the candle was joined by a second, less vibrant light. He felt his wrist grasped and held tight. A red-orange glow approached his hand. He realized it was a hot coal and tried to wrench his wrist free but it was too late. The hot coal, held by tongs, was dropped onto his palm. The dark elf dropped the tongs, which clattered on the stone, and, with his own fingers, closed Lewin's fingers around the coal. The male laughed, as Lewin struggled to open his hand and pull his wrist free.

Lewin screamed as the searing heat of the coal burned his palm and fingers. He worked his arm against the wooden edges of the opening, scraping and bruising the flesh of his forearm, but he did not register the additional pain. The burning of the coal reached down into his arm with fiery roots. The laughter of the male crescendoed.

The coal was cooling and the male grew tired of his evil sport. He released the prince's hand and wrist. Lewin dropped the offensive item and pulled his hand back through the opening.

"Smell that cooking flesh?" asked the male. "Dinner is served." He laughed, putting out the candle.

Lewin staggered backwards into the darkness, gripping his wrist, holding his hand in front of his face, although he couldn't see it.

"You trusted him?" asked an unexpected voice. He turned, peering into the darkness. He had not realized there was a second prisoner in the cell with him.

"What?"

"Did you really believe he was going to give you food?"

He recognized the voice. "You!" He backed into the wall and slumped down, holding his injured hand between his thighs.

"Let me see your hand."

"How can you see anything at all?" he shot back. He felt foolish and vulnerable at having trusted the male dark elf. He also felt disoriented and afraid. He had fallen asleep in the cave and woke up in a cell. He figured the female dark elf had somehow hastened his capture and confinement, yet here she was, in the cell with him.

"I'm a dark elf," she said. He could hear her movements. "Don't blame yourself," she added. "You have no idea the tricks they'll play. You haven't learned how to guard yourself against them." She was next to him now. She touched his upper arm. "Let me see."

"Did you press foul roots against my lips as I slept, robbing me of my wits?" he asked. "Or use magic to deepen my slumber so you could transport me here?"

"What?"

"We were in the cave. You said you could save me and yet here you have delivered me to captivity."

"You're delirious," she said. "You've been feverish, tossing and turning, ever since you were thrown in here with me. This is the first we've spoken." She reached for his forearm and gently pried his hand out of the protection of his legs. She held his wrist and looked at his hand. Lewin could not see her, only feel her touch and hear her voice.

"You defeated our army with magic, calling a blizzard to bury our soldiers and horses." He turned to her in the darkness. "You even caught your own soldiers in the ice, but cared not."

"There was a fair coating of ash on that coal." She let go of his wrist. "You were fortunate."

"Fortunate?" he shot back at her. He was going to continue his complaint but she spoke over him.

"You certainly did lose the battle, but I have no idea what magic you're talking about. I don't hear much down here, but I've overheard the guards bragging about the battle and the rather simple deception you fell for." He heard her scoot away. "I have some food. There must be plenty now, if they're feeding *me*."

He could tell by the shape of her voice that she was turned away. She scooted back to him, touched his arm, and said, "give me your *other* hand." She couldn't help but snicker when she said this. He held up his unburned hand and she placed something tough and dense in it. "Horse flesh."

"Do you know what happened to me?" he asked as he sniffed the meat. He was hungry but he didn't feel secure eating the meat. Still, he held onto it.

"I know you're Prince Lewin, now I do, anyway. I know you are the only human brought down here so far. I know you just held onto a hot coal and now you're holding onto horse meat, which you're not eating." She paused. "That's all I know about you."

"You lie!" he countered. "We met on the surface. You led me out of the blizzard, into a cave. Now you've brought me here. What I don't understand is why you're in here with me, another deception?"

"Another prisoner."

"You said that you could save me from a horrible fate," he accused her.

"Eat the meat and try to get some rest," she said, scooting away from him. Reminded of the meat, he found the solution to his growing hunger harder and harder to resist. He nibbled on the meat and tried to piece together the unbelievable events that had happened to him. Despite the cold and his discomfort, the come-down from the pain made him sleepy. Once his body began digesting the meat he was unable to stay awake.

. . .

The sounds of a thousand flies buzzing furiously about him stirred Prince Lewin from his slumber. He once more felt the soft comfort of fur against his skin. He sat up with a jolt and threw the furs off of him. He felt for his dagger, found it, and held it out. His eyes adjusted to the dim light. Little remained of the fire but burnt ends and a hill of ash, which had been spilled as the logs collapsed.

The female dark elf was sitting behind the soldier's corpse. She was as he had first seen her, in her pose of prayer, mask covering her eyes, forearms coated in congealed blood, the flies feeding. She mumbled to herself, head bent.

Lewin gathered himself into a crouch. He was in his armor. His clothing was stiff but dry. He glanced around the cave, spotting the leather bags, tools, and gear. He also saw a short spear leaned against the stone wall. He stood and made his way to the spear. He sheathed his dagger and grabbed the spear. He approached the praying dark elf and pressed the point of the spear just between her breasts.

"What's your name, witch?"

She looked up at him through the fly-eyed mask, but said nothing. He bent forward and reached for the mask. Grabbing it, he yanked it from her head and tossed it to the floor. It clattered to a stop. He regained a two-handed grip on the spear. "You're the source of the blizzard. You used magic to twist my dreams into nightmares. You let these flies feed on your blood. What kind of sorceress are you?" He shook his head, not expecting, or even wanting, an answer. "I wish we had destroyed your city and your foul race!"

She regarded him with her blood-swamped eyes and said nothing. He held the spear in place with one hand and reached down with the other. He began to unbuckle his belt. The dark elf moved her eyes, watching. A queer smile came to her face.

A terrible pain struck Lewin as he worked the belt free. He pulled his hand back and looked at it. The flesh of his palm and the pads of his fingers were blistered. He stared at his hand in disbelief.

"You flail in your sleep," said the dark elf. He looked at her. "You struck the fire."

"Lies," he whispered. "Hold out your wrists."

She did as she was told. He realized the absurdity of his command when he saw her gore and fly covered hands, wrists, and forearms. He knew the belt would slip. "Damn you, witch."

"I've already been to Hell," she said, smirking.

He bent forward, yanked the spear, and struck her in the side of the head with the wooden shaft. "Don't speak!" he yelled. "Dream twister! Fly mother! No more foul magic will cross your lips." He replaced the tip of the spear between her breasts. "Wipe the blood free."

She bent one hand towards the other, prompting him to dig the tip of the spear through the cloth of her shirt, into her flesh, lest she get ideas. With slow movements the dark elf cleaned her arms of the congealed blood. The flies swarmed and buzzed, upset by the disturbance.

He bent, and, keeping the spear against her as best he could, bound her wrists with his belt. He knew it was a haphazard restraint, especially given the slimy residue still on her skin, but it was something. He stood. "I'm taking you prisoner."

She chuckled.

He pressed the spear into her enough to halt her laughter. "It's good you brought gear. We're going to the surface. We'll make our way to Seven Rivers. I'll hold you hostage, should we come across any of your kind. Now get up." He pulled the spear back far enough for her to rise.

"Oh, foolish boy," she began. He stepped forward, spun the spear, and slammed the butt of it into her stomach. She doubled over in pain, gasping for air.

"No talking."

"Eideothea," she spat out.

For a moment Lewin feared she had spoke some foul word of power. He tensed, expecting black magic. The dark elf female rose, touching her stomach. "My name is Eideothea."

. . .

Prince Lewin kept his captive at spear point. He commanded her to gather the gear. He commanded her to relight the torch in the coals of the fire. After that, he nodded towards the tunnel and she took the lead.

"It doesn't go—" she started but the spear tip jabbed her in the small of the back, silencing her. She stepped quickly, pulling herself from the point. She mumbled the rest of her warning, "where you think it goes," but he didn't hear her. The pair began down the winding tunnel. "Seven Rivers may not even exist anymore," she observed. Prince Lewin struck her in the side of her head with the flat of the spear blade. "Ow," She reached up and touched her ear.

"No talking, witch," said Lewin. "You'll weave your spells between common words."

"I'm simply pointing out—" Again the spear. She stumbled to the side. She felt the cut on her ear and the warm blood dripping from it. The flies, tired of old wounds, took flight and followed the aroma of fresh blood. "You debase yourself, treating me cruelly," she admonished Prince Lewin. He prodded her with the spear, but with less enthusiasm. "I might also point out—"

Prince Lewin grabbed the flap of the leather satchel strung over her shoulder and yanked her to a stop. He reached over her shoulder and grabbed the front of her shirt. He pushed her to the side until she struck the tunnel wall. He pressed his fist against her chest.

"You don't need your tongue to be a valuable hostage."

Eideothea looked up at the prince. She studied the nobility of his features. She relished the stern set to his mouth and eyes. Such strength appealed to her. Prince

Lewin gleamed some understanding of her thinking. Confusion jumbled his features, then disgust. He began to release the Eideothea, but was forced to keep his grip as she spoke aloud her thinking.

"I'm not loved among my kind. Even if I was, you should know, that if a dark elf is taken hostage and used as leverage." She looked into his eyes. "The first thing we do is kill the hostage, then we kill the hostage taker." She lifted her non-torch holding hand and traced her fingers along the back of his fist, feeling the raised tendons. "Long negotiations bore us."

Lewin yanked his hand free from her touch. "Does the sickness of your people know no limit?" He turned his head. "Walk."

Eideothea pushed herself from the wall, turned, glancing at Lewin, and continued down the tunnel. "You never answered me."

"Will you never cease talking?"

She glanced over her shoulder. "Are you a virgin?" she asked. Lewin's eyes hardened.

When they reached the egg-shaped cave Lewin grabbed her shoulder. He peered past her. A shaft of blue-white light came through the opening. He prodded her forward with the spear tip. When they were below the opening he peered up into the light and snow. Eideothea looked at him.

"You'll have to decide," she said.

He turned to face her. The movement of the flies on her ear caught his attention. He glanced at them then looked back into her face. She started to continue her proposition but he surprised her. He reached out and covered her mouth with one hand. He leaned the spear against the wall then grabbed the torch from her. He lifted the torch and thrust the head into the bank of snow above.

She watched him with her blood-washed eyes. He reached without turning his eyes from her and drew his dagger.

"I'm going to remove my hand," he said. "If you open your mouth you'll find a dagger in it." He looked at her. He pulled his hand back. She looked at him, studying him. He cut free a length of cloth from his tabard. He sheathed his dagger and grabbed the back of her head, bending it forward. Eideothea knew he intended to gag her.

Before he could, she blurted out, "Wear the furs."

He paused.

"You're not dressed for the cold," she explained. He smiled, shaking his head in disbelief.

"Thanks."

"You're welcome." She opened her mouth in preparation for the gag.

He shook his head in disbelief as he placed the cloth between her teeth and tied it behind her head. The flies on her ears lifted into flight and danced around the movement of his arms. He spun her around to face away from him. He pulled the furs free from their bindings and dressed as she had advised. He spun her back around. She watched him as he checked the belt, then tightened the knot.

He looked up out of the opening. "When will this unnatural storm end?"

'Never,' she thought.

Prince Lewin looked to her, saw the gag, and smiled at his quick forgetfulness. He reached out and grabbed her left arm above the elbow. He helped her onto the ledge and then boosted her to the surface. He followed with the spear in hand. The wind was awaiting their arrival and blew with fury to greet them.

Lewin marched through the shin-high snow, head bent against the wind, dragging the dark elf female behind him. When he felt he had gone far enough out into the open, he shielded his eyes and looked around. He did not see the entrance to Pwyll. For a moment he thought it might have disappeared under ice and snow but there was nothing but a featureless white plain where he expected sloping, rocky hills.

He turned and looked in the direction of Seven Rivers. Even on a clear day he would have only been able to make out its shapes and tones but his vision was diminished by the blowing snow. Still, somehow, the land did not slope as he expected but extended out level. He turned and looked, he thought, up the foothills of the Black Ogre Mountains. He expected to see snow-topped boulders and wind-shaped stone towers but once again the featureless white plain extended.

He looked all around him. There was only white and wind. He felt disoriented and with that, he felt fear. He thought to retreat to the cave, yank Eideothea's gag, and make the witch end her hellish spell. He searched for their footprints, found them, then pulled the dark elf into motion. He followed the trail to its termination but the cave entrance could not be seen.

"What?" he asked, astonished. He released the dark elf and knelt down in the snow. He began to search the snow for the cave entrance. Finding nothing he turned to Eideothea. "Where—" But she was gone. He regained his feet and looked all around. There was no sight of the dark elf. He looked to the snow. The wind, gusting, erased their tracks. It was as if he had been dropped in this very spot.

Having no feature to place his hope on, no direction being any more promising than any other, Prince Lewin chose to head towards where he believed Seven

Rivers to be. He could not trust his senses, he thought, but perhaps he could trust his feet.

Prince Lewin was strong, disciplined, and even had the benefit of furs, but no man can long stand the frozen plain, the relentless assault of the wind, and the omnipresent cold. He was half-unconscious when he finally collapsed.

. . .

Eideothea caught up to Lewin, leaving his belt and gag far behind in the snow. She dropped to her knees next to him. She rolled him onto his back, so that his face was no longer buried in the snow. She understood the cold and how to endure it. She knew Lewin was in danger. She dropped the packs from her shoulders, pulled one in front of her, and began to dig amongst the tools.

She pulled a folded, saw-toothed blade free and unfolded it, locking it in place with a pin. She rose and stepped to the side. She bent and began to saw the thick floor of snow into blocks. These she stacked as she went along, forming a circular wall around Lewin's unconscious body.

"You—," muttered Lewin.

Eideothea turned from the cutting, set the saw down, and knelt over him.

"You—" he repeated. He stirred and tried to sit up but collapsed back onto the snow.

She leaned closer to him and intended to comfort him with her words but he surprised her. He reached up and grabbed the collar of her fur cloak. He yanked against her and brought himself up, smashing his forehead against her face. The blow forced her from his grasp. She doubled over backwards.

Prince Lewin rolled over and began to crawl away from the dark elf. He tried to stand, crashed through an unexpected low wall of snow, and faltered. Snow flew from the shattered blocks and blinded him. He stopped and shook his head, casting off the snowy mask. This made him dizzy. The bright white of the trackless plain faded to darkness. He felt the blood run from his head. His legs failed him. Once again, he was face down in the snow.

Eideothea reached up and touched her face. When she pulled her hand back there was fresh blood. She could feel her left eye swelling shut. The blow, so unexpected and hard, stirred stars in her vision. Still, being a dark elf, she had been struck in the face many times. She knew she had to think past the pain.

She pictured the spear and Lewin rising over her to drive it home. This forced her into action. She rolled onto her side and looked for Lewin. When she saw him lying face-down in the snow she calmed. She allowed herself a moment to nurse her pain, resting the injured side of her face on the snow. For a few moments the cold forced the pain and swelling away. Then it introduced its own hurt.

She stood and walked to Lewin. She turned him over once again, picked up the saw, and began to cut fresh blocks. He did not stir again as she completed the domed shelter of snow. She crouched in the snow and stripped herself bare. The flies she had been sheltering flew about, exploring the space and the fresh cut along her cheekbone. She used her furs to make a pallet.

She bent over Lewin, opened his furs and stripped him. She crawled on top of him and pulled her own furs over them to trap their shared heat. She worked her hands slowly over his chilled flesh, using friction to work the life-heat back into him. He stirred and muttered half-formed words from the edge of consciousness.

"Shhh, you're at death's door, my valiant prince. Don't enter that bleak house."

The flies buzzed in the air above them. Eideothea snaked her arm through the furs, forming a little tunnel of entrance. When the flies saw her ebony-skinned hand against the backdrop of white they swarmed together and angled their flight to her. They crawled down the familiar flesh of her arm onto her shoulder and breasts. They found in that dark, warm shelter a new body. They began to explore it with curiosity.

"Baalzebul favors you," she whispered into his ear. "Do you feel his caress?" He moaned, recognizing her presence and touch, but was not cognizant of her words. "Accept his charity. Accept his truth," she advised. "Baalzebul," she said in reverent tones, "Lord of the Seventh, Hell's greatest Angel, He Who is Victorious. Accept him. Accept him." Her litany wove itself into his mind as he drifted deeper into unconsciousness.

. . .

The sound of the rusty hinges woke him. He opened his eyes. A dark elf male stood in the doorway, lit by candlelight. Prince Lewin looked around the cell and found her. She was curled up against the wall. He could barely make out her shape in the feeble light.

"Stop it!" he screamed at her. "End your spell, witch!" She woke and half turned. The dark elf male stepped into the room, laughing.

"What do you want from me?" asked Prince Lewin, directing his question to Eideothea. She looked at him, then turned her eyes to the dark elf male. Lewin saw a look of alarm cross her features. He looked at the guard, just in time to see the man motion towards the door. Several other guards rushed into the cell.

One guard stood in front of Lewin, a short sword in his hand, pointed at the prince. Two other guards went to Eideothea. Knowing what was coming, she curled up in a defensive ball. The guards began kicking her. One reached down and began to pry her out of her clenched position. He rolled her onto her back, knelt on top of her, pinning her down with a knee in her gut, and held her arms apart. He said something to his companion in the dark elf language. The second guard bent forward and struck Eideothea in the face. She turned her head, trying to shield herself, as he hit her again.

"What are you doing?" cried Prince Lewin. "Stop! Leave her alone!" He reflexively moved toward her. The dark elf with the short sword growled at him and pressed the tip of the sword against his chest.

"Stop what? We aren't doing anything?" argued the male guard with the candle.

Lewin looked to him. "You're beating her! Why?"

The sounds of violence filled the small cell: the grunting of the men, the thuds of their boots and fists on Eideothea's unprotected body, her cries of pain.

The dark elf guard with the candle stepped closer to Lewin. "You're doing this!" he screamed. "You have the gall to blame us, when it's you who reject him?"

"Who?" cried Lewin.

Eideothea screamed as the guards struck her.

"Enough!" said the guard. "You'll kill her. He doesn't want that, not yet, not unless she fails." The guards beating Eideothea stood panting over her. She curled up, not in defense, but in pain. Her agonized moaning undercut the guard's words.

"Look what you've done by rejecting him." The guard shook his head as the other men passed behind him, exiting the cell. "Like any father, he can be merciful," said the male. "All he asks for is love and devotion." The male backed towards the door. "When you spurn him, when you deny his love, when the child fails the father, what's left?" He glanced towards Eideothea. "Wrath." He blew out the candle and shut the door.

Lewin crawled to Eideothea. He reached out and touched her. She had stopped moaning. "Eideothea?" He wasn't sure why he had concern for her. Perhaps, he thought, it was the suddenness and violence of the unexpected attack that called upon his natural empathy and concern for others. "Eideothea? Are you—" But he needn't finish his question. She couldn't hear him. She had passed out from the pain.

He lay next to her and placed a protective arm around her. "I won't let them do that again," he whispered to her. He held her until exhaustion took him.

. . .

Prince Lewin tossed and turned. He was hot. There was pressure on him. There was a nuisance on his flesh. He struggled to awaken. He felt pain and hunger. These sharp things stirred him.

"Shhh, Prince," whispered Eideothea. She rest her head next to his, her face turned to him. Her lips caressed the skin of his neck as she spoke. He let the warm, soft presence push him back into the peace and quiet of sleep.

. . .

Prince Lewin awoke in the darkness. He was cold and shivering. He was holding something, 'no, someone,' he realized. The darkness was total but he knew from touch he was holding Eideothea. His left arm was trapped beneath her waist and the stone floor. He pulled it free and used his elbow to prop himself up.

'The cell,' he thought.

He could feel the rags he wore. Gone were the furs. He began to disentangle his right arm from Eideothea's crossed-arm-grip. She stirred and pulled his arm against her, mumbling something in her native tongue. He paused his movement, feeling a twang of guilt at the prospect of waking her. He frowned at his own thinking. He yanked his arm free and scooted away from her. He sat with his back against the wall. He could hear her legs move, scrapping the floor, as she curled up in an attempt to keep hold of the shared warmth.

"When will you end this nightmare?" he asked. She moved in the darkness. "Do you delight in being both the cause of, and partner to, my misery?"

"I told you—"

"Yes, you can save me," he interrupted. "You also said you had taken me to Cocytus, where neither dark elf nor demon could find me."

"—I'm a fellow prisoner," she finished.

"Prince Lewin!"

The candlelight reappeared in the small rectangular slot in the door. The male looked through the opening. "Move to the wall, away from the other prisoner."

Lewin heard the jangle of keys. He heard the scrape of the iron bar. The door opened. The dark elf male stepped into the cell. Lewin thought to charge him, to tackle him and beat him into unconsciousness.

"Get up!" the dark elf yelled. He grabbed Lewin by the arm and lifted him to his feet. Lewin found that it was difficult to keep his balance. Without the jailer's "help" he would have fallen, weakened by hunger, fatigue, and stress. The dark elf drug him to the wall of the cell, pressed his back against the stone.

Eideothea turned her face into the candlelight. Lewin saw that the entire left side of her face was swollen. The flesh around her left eye was puffy. A dull red scab extended down the ridge of her cheek bone.

The guard brought his face close to Lewin's. "If you try to interfere, it will be much worse."

Lewin looked into the male's face. He shifted his gaze to a pair of males that entered the cell through the open door. The second male to enter was pulling on a pair of skin-tight gloves.

"Strip her," commanded the male with the candle.

"What are you—" began Lewin.

The dark elf guard smiled. "Show him."

The male with the gloves turned and stepped up to Lewin. The other male cornered Eideothea and began to grab at her rags, despite her protest and scrambling. Lewin looked from the guard with the candle to the struggle in the corner.

The gloved guard brought his hands, palm up, into view. Something sparkled in the candle light on the palm and fingers of his gloves. Lewin looked down. Dozens of metal shards pierced the skin of each glove. The guard smiled and lowered his hands. "You're going to flay her." Said the guard with the candle.

"Me?" gasped Lewin.

"It's because you reject him," argued the guard. "He lashes out because he's hurt. This is your doing."

The two guards ripped the rags from Eideothea. The bare-handed guard lifted to her feet and held her immobile, arms pinned behind her back. The jutting bones of her emaciated body reflected the candlelight in glowing, angular planes. The shard-gloved guard stood in front of her, palms out.

"Don't!" cried Lewin. He pushed against the guard restraining him. The guard dropped his arm. A dagger hidden in his sleeve fell into his hand. He pressed the point into Lewin's abdomen. "I'll gut you."

Lewin tried to twist to the side, but the dagger dug into his flesh. He paused and looked into the guard's face. The high cheekbones and narrow jaw caught the flickering light, giving the face a hard-edged appearance, as if his features were not composed of curved forms, but of steel, like the shards in the flaying gloves.

"Then we'll have our fun with her."

A cry from Eideothea caught Lewin's attention. He looked from the guard to her.

The shard-gloved guard stepped forward. He grabbed her breasts with his hands and squeezed them. As Lewin watched he clinched his hands into fists. He yanked his hands towards his hips. Eideothea tried to bend with his movement but the guard holding her pulled her erect. Even in the weak light, Lewin saw blood spray against the wall, floor, and gloved guard. Lewin looked away.

"No, no, that won't do," muttered the guard pinning him against the wall with his dagger. "You need to watch."

"I won't be witness to your cruelty," countered Lewin. "Nor am I the cause of it!"

"You'll watch," said the male in a low voice. "Or we will flay every piece of skin from her and leave her in your arms to die."

Lewin returned his eyes to Eideothea. The candlelight reflected off of the slick of blood traveling downwards from the valley between her breasts to the edge of her concave stomach.

The gloved guard reached down with his right hand, sliding his fingers against Eideothea's pubic mound. She pressed her thighs together to prevent him from moving his hand lower. The guard behind her began to work his knee between her thighs from behind. The gloved guard laughed, placed his palms against her thighs, and drug the shards of metal across her unprotected skin. She cried out in pain.

"Enough!" screamed Lewin. "Enough! What do you want?" The gloved guard paused his movement. Lewin looked to the guard pinning him to the wall. "You want me to accept him? Is that it? I accept! Do you hear me? I accept? I accept."

"Do you now?" purred the guard. He glanced over his shoulder. "Did I tell you to stop?"

Lewin brought his arm across his body, knocking the dark elf's hand, and the dagger it held, to the side. He pushed himself from the wall and dodged past the startled guard. The two dark elves tormenting Eideothea turned and looked. Lewin rushed the man with the gloves. He swung at him. The guard twisted to the side, evading the blow, but Lewin's momentum carried him into the guard. The two men slammed into the stone wall.

The second guard threw Eideothea to the floor and stepped over her. As Lewin and the gloved guard tangled their arms and bodies, the second guard grabbed Lewin's shoulder from behind. He half spun the prince, partially extracting him from his wild grapple. Lewin turned his face just in time to meet the fist coming at him. He saw stars, then darkness.

· · ·

"Lewin! Wake up!"

He opened his eyes and looked into Eideothea's face. She was holding up the edge of the furs, letting light in. He could see that the swelling on the left side of her face had gone down. She had, however, picked the scab from the cut on her cheek. Several flies lined the edges, drinking.

Lewin became aware that he was naked, that she was naked on top of him, and that flies were crawling back and forth on their exposed flesh. He tried to disentangle himself from her, to find his way out of the furs. He paused his frantic actions as memories flooded over him.

"The cell," he breathed. "They were flaying you. I —" He glanced down at her breasts but could not see them. They were pressed against his chest and hidden by shadow. He again began to squirm out from under her.

"Don't," she advised him. "This is the only way to stay warm." She lowered the edge of the furs. Only a dim glow crept into their cocoon. "You've were mostly dead, then, eventually, half alive." She smiled, "I saved you from freezing to death—again."

"The cell?"

"Fever dream."

He looked at her in the gloom. "Cocytus?"

"Yes."

"There is no cell?" he asked. "No dark elves tormenting us?"

"You are far from Pwyll."

"I dream of it?" he asked, more of himself than her. "So real," he whispered. "I was in a cell." He studied her face in the gloom. "We were in a cell. It's too real to be a dream. Your face." He realized his hand was against her body. He felt the pain of the puffy blisters on his palm. "The burn on my hand, from the coal."

"From the logs."

"Let me see your breasts, your thighs," he demanded.

She turned her face from his.

"If you have cuts—" His voice trailed. He realized that he didn't know what it would mean if she had cuts. 'Would it mean that *this* is the dream?' he asked himself.

"You have to eat and drink," she advised. "You've been standing at death's door."

"Which is real?" he asked. "Which is real and which is the lie? They can't both be true." She began to rise. He tried to grip her, hold her in place, but she was slippery with sweat. She rose into a crouch, spinning away from him, pulling the fur around her. Lewin at once felt the chill air attack his skin.

He rose into a crouch and began to pull the winter wear into place. As he did so he noticed a wash of blood on his chest. He looked over his body. He saw that his thighs were also pink with the mixture of blood and sweat.

Then he noticed it. The red divot in his abdomen. 'The guard's dagger,' he thought.

"Look at me," he commanded Eideothea.

She paused in her dressing and looked over her shoulder.

"This wound." He glanced down at his stomach. He looked back to her. "The guard's dagger."

Eideothea turned away. She pulled the furs into place. "I have rations and water. We have to eat, then we have to move."

"I'm not going anywhere."

"Then you'll die on the frozen plain." She turned on her knees to face him. The cloud of flies buzzed around the pair.

Lewin stared into her blood-filled eyes.

"I accepted him," he stated. "I told the guard that I accepted him, so they would stop hurting you."

Eideothea studied his face, without speaking.

"Let me see your breasts," he said, his voice gentler then before. "If you don't, I won't trust you. I won't travel with you. I'll take my chances."

"You'll die."

"Then I'll die."

Eideothea frowned. "I didn't know humans were so stubborn." She reached up and pulled open her furs, exposing her breasts. Lewin looked from her large, blood-washed eyes, to her small, pert breasts. They too were washed with blood. Scores of parallel red cuts seeped blood. As he studied her breasts, blood ran to her cold-erected nipples, formed twin teardrops, and fell onto the fur.

"The cell is real," murmured Lewin. "This is the lie." He looked into her face. "The guard did that. I saw it happen."

Eideothea closed her fur coat. "No," she countered. "I did this to myself." She studied him. "You were on the edge of death. You were feverish and delirious, but you were still aware enough to notice my actions, on some level." She paused, studying him. "If there is a deception it is you deceiving yourself."

"Why?" he asked. "Why would you do that to yourself?"

A slow smile crossed her face. "For you."

He looked at her, not understanding.

"So he would show you kindness."

"Who?" he asked.

"My master."

"Who is your master?"

"Baalzebul, the Lord of Flies. He fed on my blood. He accepted my offering. Death did *not* take you."

"A lie!" His anger filled the small, domed space. He lowered his voice to a harsh whisper. "I have the guard's cut."

"I did that to you."

"You lie!"

She looked into his eyes. "Our blood had to mingle; he had to taste you, taste us, before he would agree. I used your dagger. Look at it."

He dug through his furs and found his dagger sheath. He pulled the blade free and looked at the tip. The metal was rose-colored. He looked from the dagger to her, then back to the tip of the blade. He was uncertain. 'Is this from before? From her?' He asked himself. He tried to recall if he had drawn her blood. If he had, he tried to recall if he had wiped the blade clean. He could not remember.

"A trick," he whispered.

"For what purpose?" She reached out and touched his hand. Her flesh was warm. He looked down. He was struck by the sharp contrast of her ebony skin at the center of so much whiteness, his own skin, and the background of snow and ice. "I helped you. Just as you helped me," she said. He looked up at her. "You said you negotiated with the guards, gave them what they wanted, to end my suffering."

"You say that isn't real."

"The sentiment is the same. The self-sacrifice." She smiled, looking down at her own chest.

"Is that how you—" He looked into her scabbed face, her red eyes. "Saved me from my horrible fate? By mingling our blood and offering it to, what's his name, Baalzebul?"

"We need to eat," she said, "then move, before a blizzard overtakes us. What the ice takes, the ice keeps."

"Is there no where safe?"

"Yes."

"Where?"

"My master's house."

. . .

Eideothea knocked open the exit of the igloo and crawled out. Prince Lewin followed. The frozen plain extended to the horizon in three directions. In the fourth, a ridge of ice and stone rose from snow to sky. There was little wind, the blizzard had ended while they slept, but the sky swirled with towering, grey-bottomed clouds.

Eideothea helped him to his feet. "Do you want to gag me?" she asked. "Or bind me?" she added, playfully. Lewin looked at her as he pulled up his fur hood. "Maybe you want the spear again?" She smiled as she pulled her fly-eyed goggles into place. She picked up the pack and slung it over her shoulder. She turned and headed towards the rise of ice and stone.

Despite the threatening skies there was little wind. The ground was ice with a dusting of snow. This made every step a hazard yet the pair, under Eideothea's leadership, kept a good pace. The rations, salted meat and a biscuit as hard as stone, kept his hunger pangs at bay. Lewin kept his head bent down, his eyes squinted against the glare, and focused his attention on Eideothea's footfalls. He walked where she walked.

"There's many types of snow," she said, speaking over her shoulder. "The surface, I mean. It all depends on the humidity, the temperature, the wind. Some snow is easier to walk on than other types. We're lucky, this isn't bad. I've...."

As she spoke his mind wandered. He thought of the cell, of their shared captivity and torture. He asked himself if it was real. He replayed every memory he had since waking up in the snow. He attempted to sort out what was real and what must be deception. He studied Eideothea's face, the inflection of her words, searching for falsehood or truth.

Despite all of his attempts nothing seemed completely real or trustworthy. Soon his physical fatigue returned, as did his hunger. His investigations became an activity he could not afford. He bent all of his energies to lifting one foot and then the other. He realized, after an indeterminable amount of time following Eideothea through the white-on-white terrain, that he had come to depend on her, more than that, he needed her to survive.

. . .

Ice and stone rose sharply in front of them. Eideothea guided him into a steep, blue-walled crevasse in the ice. She seemed to know the terrain. She turned from the initial ravine into a second crevasse that branched from the first. Here she sat on a rock gripped by the ice and rested. He sat next to her.

Blue walls of ice rose in front of and behind them. The ice held massive black stones in its eternal grip. The sky above was filled with various shades of blue, ranging from pale, milky blue to black. Over this backdrop rode puffy white clouds with grey bottoms. Overall, however, the light had not changed.

"How long until nightfall?" he asked.

She was digging in the pack and did not answer. She pulled out more rations and divided them between them. She produced a water skin from deep within the folds of her furs, where it was kept from freezing. "There's no day or night here. It is always thus." She lifted and hand to her goggles, raised them to her forehead, and glanced up at the sky.

He looked from her to the sky. He saw no sun, no concentration of light in the sky. "Cocytus," he said, looking around. He studied the ice and stones. "Is this really Hell, as you say?"

She nodded.

"Hell is fire and burning," he protested.

"Cold burns," she stated between chews. "Drink." She handed him the water skin.

"You've been here before?"

She nodded.

"You worship a devil?" He took the water skin, pulled the cap, lifted it to his lips, and poured the rapidly cooling water into his parched mouth.

"Most dark elves worship demons, from the Abyss." She took the water skin back from his extended hand and tucked it back into her furs.

"I don't know the difference."

She shrugged her shoulders. "It's not worth troubling over."

"You want me to accept your master, a devil?"

She looked sidelong at him. "You said you already had." She winked at him, her ebony eyelid, with its white eyelashes, flashed over her blood red eye. Lewin was struck by the oddity of it.

"I—"

"Don't worry, an oath made in duress, or," she looked away from him, "in an altered state, is not a binding oath."

He began to inquire about the cell, about the captivity. It seemed so real, and in it she was present, so it followed she could answer to the particulars. He stopped, realizing she would know nothing other than what he had told her. 'That is,' he concluded, 'if she is to be believed.' He looked from her to the ice and rock. 'If *this* is to be believed.'

Eideothea stood. She pulled the spear from its resting place on the stone and held it out in front of her, towards the entrance to the crevasse. Her body was tense, ready for action. He reached into his furs, finding the dagger. A shadow fell over the opening. Lewin turned.

A massive creature appeared. It clung to the ice at the top of the crevasse, being too large to squeeze itself lower. Both Eideothea and Lewin looked up at it. The creature was unlike anything Lewin had ever seen. At first glance it appeared to be an enormous insect, something like a praying mantis. As he studied it the differences became apparent.

It clung to the ice with two sets of jointed legs that ended in single claws. Like a praying mantis, its frontmost pair of legs folded down, allowing it to grapple its prey. Its abdomen and thorax were covered with thick white fur that completely coated and hid its cuticle plates. The thorax was elongated and jointed so that the creature could hold its fore-body erect. It tilted its head and looked at them with twin, compound eyes.

Lewin saw movement at the periphery of his vision. He glanced and saw Eideothea lower her compound eyed goggles into place. Lewin looked back to the creature above them. It tilted its head and regarded Eideothea. Or so it appeared, without pupils, it was difficult to tell where it was focusing its attention.

The creature, 'It must be nearly twenty feet long,' thought Lewin, began to click its mandibles. The sound echoed off of the ice. Lewin heard a second clicking, although softer than the first. He realized it was Eideothea and looked at her. She was mimicking the sound. The creature seemed satisfied with her response and began to crawl back into the wider crevasse from which it came.

"Are we—"

"Come on," commanded Eideothea. She grabbed Lewin by the arm and pulled him to his feet.

"We're not going with that—thing?"

"Yes." Eideothea watched both her footing and the creature above them.

"By the gods, what is it?"

"A gelugon," she whispered. "Powerful," she added, with awe.

Lewin leaned in, whispering in her ear. "It's massive."

She glanced from the gelugon to Lewin. A wry smile spread over her face. "Its rather small, for a gelugon." She raised a finger to her lips, indicating Lewin should restrain from any further comments or questions.

The gelugon led them through the maze of broken ice. Finally, it arrived at the edge of the glacier. The crevasse terminated at a towering wall of black stone. The gelugon climbed from the ice to the stone, disappearing over the top. Eideothea knelt and dropped the pack from her shoulders.

"Now what?"

"We climb." Eideothea opened the pack and pulled two pairs of crampons free. These were followed by something like small picks. "Are you afraid of heights?" she asked, looking up.

Lewin looked from the tools to the sheer wall. "What if I am?" he asked, his voice hollow. Eideothea chuckled. She sat and began to strap the crampons to her boots.

. . .

The gelugon was waiting for them at the top. As Eideothea helped pull Lewin over the edge he glanced up at the towering insect. He wished he hadn't. He scooted away from the edge, closer to the gelugon, and began to remove his crampons. The gelugon clicked and Eideothea responded. Their conversation went on for some time, as if they were debating something.

Lewin could see little of the plateau past the gelugon's body. He turned and looked out over the glacier, then past it, to the plain below. He realized that the plain was actually a frozen lake, or even, perhaps, a sea. Until he saw the vast expanse, he had been consoling himself that he was still outside of Pwyll, lost somewhere in the desert, the sand and stone hidden by ice and snow. Now, that comforting lie had been shattered by the truth.

He was in Cocytus, a frozen corner of Hell.

He was struck by the profound realization that Pwyll and Seven Rivers; which, also meant his father's kingdom, and with it, his home, were all impossibly far away. He looked to Eideothea. 'I'm completely dependent on her,' he thought. 'She holds my life in her hands. A dark elf. My enemy.' He looked to the gelugon. 'A devil worshipper.'

The dialogue of clicks between Eideothea and the gelugon became furious. Lewin could tell from Eideothea's body language that the two were engaged in an argument.

The thought of it filled him with fear. He assumed that the gelugon, small or not, could easily kill them. He could not fathom why she would argue with such a creature.

The beating of his heart began to quicken. He felt the need to take some self-preserving action. He had the fear-inspired thought of scrambling back down the ice, to the bottom of the crevasse, where the gelugon could not fit. He then remembered that his crampons and the climbing pick had been packed away. He looked from Eideothea to the gelugon. He knew there was nothing he could do.

Eideothea waved her arm in a signal of defeat. She turned. Lewin saw that her mouth was twisted in disgust. The gelugon rose erect, turned, and began to slowly and awkwardly walk forward.

"Greedy," Eideothea muttered to herself.

"I'm glad it didn't kill us," admitted Lewin.

Eideothea lifted her goggles and looked at him with her blood-soaked eyes. "I doubt he would get away with it." She turned her head and looked at the retreating gelugon. "He saw an opportunity to threaten, that's all." She looked back to Lewin. "I promised him a future boon. I paid him off, in effect, to convince him to carry on with his duties."

Lewin didn't know what to say. He looked from Eideothea to the gelugon. The dialogue, even though he had witnessed it, was impossible to comprehend.

"He leads, we follow," said Eideothea, as she picked up the pack.

. . .

Although the gelugon's legs were much longer, his manner of walking was laborious and slow. It was easy to keep up with him. Lewin scanned the plateau. It was ringed with mountains of snow-capped black stone. One of the mountains, far to Lewin's left, emitted a column of black smoke. The wind carried the smoke high above the mountains, spreading it over the peaks like a think blanket of black wool.

Lewin had to squint his eyes to block out the light. He followed the jagged line of the peaks that separated sky from ground. He paused, realizing there was something above the peak directly in front of them, something obscured by the volcano's sky-borne ash. All he could discern was its rough diamond shape and its deep black color.

A wind picked up, racing down from the mountain. Both he and Eideothea gathered closer behind the gelugon. His massive body partially shielded them. Lewin bowed his head, allowing the fur of his hood to bear the brunt of the wind. He lifted his hand and covered his lower face with his glove.

He marched without thinking. It was too cold for the working of the mind. Several times he thoughtlessly veered from behind the gelugon. A blast of cold wind greeted him, advising him to correct course. After a seemingly endless march the gelugon stopped. Prince Lewin lifted his head and looked around.

Foothills of black stone reached up from the snow and ice. Before these rose a narrow field of wind-carved ice crags. The image of the flaying gloves, their metal shards glinting in the candlelight, sprang from Lewin's memory, sending a shiver down his spine. He realized that both Eideothea and the gelugon were staring at him. He looked self-consciously from one to the other.

The gelugon turned and looked up. He extended his leg and unfurled his pincer, pointing. Prince Lewin followed the motion. He could better make out the object hovering above the peaks. It appeared to be an enormous piece of rock, large enough to support a city, held aloft by some unknown force. A collection of ice-encrusted chains dropped from the bottom of the stone and disappeared behind the peaks. 'If I can see them at this distance,' thought Lewin, 'they must be truly massive.' The gelugon's clicking returned Lewin's attention to the creature.

"The Lofty House," translated Eideothea. Lewin looked to her, then back up to the chain-held rock.

"He will take us no further," said Eideothea. "You must lead us from here."

"Me?" asked Lewin.

The gelugon leapt into the air. A pair of wings opened, raining snow down on Eideothea and Lewin. The gelugon buzzed overhead, riding the outgoing winds. With the creature no longer providing cover, the wind bit into Lewin's exposed skin. He turned his back to it. "How should I know where to go?" he yelled over the howling of the wind.

"There's a cave ahead," advised Eideothea.

"So, lead us there."

"A path cuts through the crags. You must lead the way."

The wind blew down her hood. Her hair wiped about her face. She seemed unconcerned. Lewin frowned. He preferred the shelter of a cave to the exposure of the open air. 'If she wants me to lead, so be it,' he thought. He turned and began towards the opening in the ribbon of ice.

The crags lifted the wind above them, allowing for a relative calm. Lewin kept his eyes on the path. He realized that Eideothea was falling behind. He turned to her. She was standing some distance behind him, her fly-eyed goggles in her hand, looking at him. He waved her forward. She did not move or acknowledge his gesture.

'What's wrong with her?' he wondered. He heard a dull thud to his right. He realized the sound had been at the edge of his awareness since he began to walk among the crags. He looked from Eideothea to the ice crag beside him. It was perhaps twice as tall as him, thicker at the base then at the tip, like a stalagmite of ice rising from the white floor.

At first he saw nothing except the shimmering surface of blue-white. The thudding grew louder. He glanced at Eideothea. Her expression was unchanged. He returned his attention to the crag. A shadow seemed to pass over and through the ice. He stepped closer. He saw a man. It was the soldier who had been trapped under the ice outside of Pwyll. He ran the rest of the distance. He lifted his fur-gloved hands and placed them against the ice.

'Yes, it's him!' Lewin thought.

"I'll get you out." He turned to Eideothea. "Come here!" he yelled. He pointed to the pack. "I need the ice pick! Hurry." He turned back to the trapped soldier. As before, the soldier was banging his fist against the ice. "I'll break you out!" yelled Lewin. He turned and stepped towards Eideothea. "Hurry!"

She did not move. Lewin looked to the trapped soldier and motioned that the man should remain patient. The pained pleading in the man's eyes troubled him. Lewin ran down the path to Eideothea.

"I need the pack," he said, reaching for the bag. Eideothea dropped her shoulder back, moving the strap of the bag out of Lewin's reach. She eyed him, the feature of her face hard, her blood-soaked eyes merciless. This gave him pause. Eideothea looked from him to the closest crag of ice. Lewin followed her gaze.

'Another soldier!' He turned and looked at a third spike of ice. It too acted as a prison. He spun and stepped to yet another crag. He lifted his hand and wiped the snow from the folds of ice. A man's face, his eyes filled with panic, looked out from the ice. Lewin stumbled backwards.

"My father's men," he gasped. He turned to Eideothea. "You knew."

She looked from the crag to him.

"That's why you wanted me to lead the way. To shock me."

"To educate you."

"How many?" he asked, his voice trembling.

"As many as I could get beneath the ice."

"Why?"

"To honor Baalzebul."

Lewin advanced towards Eideothea, intent on the pack and the picks within. He grabbed the pack.

"You can't free them—that way."

She willingly let the pack pass from her to him. He reached into it and pulled free an ice pick. He walked back to the ice crag that imprisoned the soldier he had now seen twice. He lifted the pick and brought it down against the ice. With a sharp crack the tip of the pick broke, spun high into the air, arcing over and behind him, and disappeared amongst the crags. He turned to Eideothea.

"How?" He rushed her, grabbed her by the front of her fur coat, and pulled her close.

"Their fates have not yet been decided."

"They're locked in unbreakable ice." He jerked her body. "You said—"

"I owe an offering," she stated. "The souls of your father's men would please my master."

"Souls," echoed Lewin. He glanced to the ice crag to his right. The man within stood morose, his eyes vacant.

"Unless I can offer him something—else."

Lewin looked back to her. "Me?"

He pushed her away, waving the broken ice pick between them. "That's blackmail," he countered. "You said an oath given under duress—"

Eideothea stepped towards him. Her features softened. "All I ask is that you grant him an honest audience. Listen to him. Hear his words with an open mind."

"If I refuse? You'll give him—"

"I ask so little," said Eideothea. "I ask you only to listen." She paused, giving Lewin a space to speak. He remained silent. "If only you'll hear him out, perhaps," she looked to the crags.

"You're evil," stated Prince Lewin. "You condemn these honest men."

"Do I?" She stepped closer to Lewin. "How did these men come to me? Who sent them? Who condemned them?"

Lewin looked into her blood-soaked eyes. "They were brave men, loyal men."

"They were tools. Your father knows that. Your father sent these men to face a foe he knew was capable of —" She let her words go unspoken.

"You accuse my father—"

"Of being a king," interjected Eideothea. "Of being a ruler."

"Of being evil! He isn't! He's not like you!"

"No, Prince Lewin," countered Eideothea, her tone gentle. "He didn't send those men to fight a demonic foe because he was foolish or callous, but because he was wise."

Lewin looked at her.

"To lead means to accept a terrible responsibility." She stepped up to Lewin and placed her hands on his shoulders. "Your father sent you so you could lead, to show you, the terrible blade that hangs over the throne. It is not a comfortable chair to occupy."

"My father—"

"He can't help you," interjected Eideothea. "He can't help these men now. He can't save their souls." Lewin looked down into her blood-washed eyes. "*You* can, Lewin. You can lead. Baalzebul led the army of fallen angels as they stormed Heaven's gate. It was Baalzebul's wisdom that freed the multitudes from the yoke of their oppressor. He can teach you. He can fill you with the wisdom of his experience."

"A devil?" whispered prince Lewin. "A—fallen angel."

The fear and helplessness captured in Lewin's contorted features, held in the freezing tears welling up in his eyes, caused Eideothea to hold her counter-argument. She pressed her cheek against his chest.

"Share my warmth, let me share yours." She looked up at him. She identified his vulnerability. She grabbed his hand in hers and led him to the cave. He followed her without looking up. He couldn't bring himself to meet the gazes of the trapped men.

. . .

Lewin was thankful for her warmth. He lay with her, skin-to-skin, in the furs. The flies crawled from her to him, as before, but he hardly noticed their activity. He could not see her. He knew her only by touch. By the curves of her feminine form pressing down on him.

He traced his fingers along her back. He defined the shape of her muscle with his touch. His fingers ran over something rough. A scabbed-over cut. He gingerly explored the cut. It was little more than a scratch, really, and seemed harmless. As he touched her wound he realized she was kissing his chest.

He remembered her question, 'Are you a virgin?' He lifted his other hand and placed it on the small of her back. He felt the twin dimples on either side of her spine. The bottom of his palm felt the rise of her muscles, as they lifted and formed the curve of her butt. She partially lifted and he felt her erect nipples brush against him. She wiggled her body up his. He knew she was searching for his lips with her own.

He turned his head to the side. He dropped his hands from her body. "Why do you torment me?"

"Most men consider this pleasure, not torment."

"You are a dark elf witch. A devil worshipper. You've trapped men's souls. Now you tempt me."

She paused. He could feel her smile. "You were willing enough to lie with me."

"Survival."

"Just survival?" She reached down and picked up his hand. He did not pull away. She guided his hand onto her butt. She moved his hand over her. After allowing it for a moment, Lewin jerked his hand away. Eideothea sighed. She rest her head on his chest. She could hear the pounding of his heart. She could feel the conflict in him. "How old is your father?"

Lewin did not answer.

"You are his only son, his heir."

"Am I?"

"Lewin," She lifted her head to look at his face, although he could not see hers. "We have spies in your father's court." He turned his head to face her. "I know you are his heir. He sent you to Pwyll because he expected victory. He wanted you to return to the capital on the wings of glory." She set her cheek against the muscles of his chest.

"I failed him," whispered Lewin. "I failed those men out there." He lifted his arms and wrapped them around Eideothea's thin waist. He clutched her close, finding comfort in her presence, despite everything he knew about her.

"Your father miscalculated," she said. "He underestimated us."

"When kings error—"

"Men die," finished Eideothea. "His defeat will shake the people's confidence in him," continued Eideothea. "The people worry about you. My people gloat. They were quick to communicate that they held you prisoner—for a time." She could feel Lewin's eyes on her. "The stability of your father's rule is in doubt. The heir is gone. People hate uncertainty more than anything else."

"I'm not dead. I'm not gone. I'm captured." Despite knowing he should feel anger and resentment, he didn't. He traced his fingers along Eideothea's hips, crossed his arms, lifted them, and touched the jutting blades of her shoulders. "An honest audience?"

"That's all he asks of you," said Eideothea.

"And the men?" He struggled over his words, "their souls."

"Their fates have not yet been decided."

"Until I decide," concluded Prince Lewin. "And if I reject him? Is that the horrible fate you spoke of?"

Eideothea did not answer. Instead, she resumed her gentle kissing. Lewin did not protest. The brush of her lips electrified his skin. He felt a wave of energy work its way through his flesh, sending his blood to the surface as goose-pimples. He shuddered. Eideothea sprang forward. Her face hovered just above his. He could feel her breath on his face. He could feel the moisture of her mouth close to his.

He feared her kiss but he didn't turn away from it. Eideothea leaned closer. He lifted his head. The edge of their lips touched. Eideothea pulled back. She extended her tongue and licked his lips. "Have you been saving yourself for a princess?"

He tried to kiss her but she pulled back further. This confused him. He felt unsure of himself, of her. He set his head back against the furs. She leaned forward and touched her lips to his once more. She drug her lips over his, spreading her moisture to him.

"An arranged marriage," he answered. "A wife, to produce an heir."

"A queen?" She took his top lip between her teeth and bit down, not hard enough to draw blood, but enough to cause pain. Lewin turned his head, freeing his lip. He immediately turned his head back.

'I'll be king.' The thought never felt so real as it did now. He wondered, 'will I? Will I ever escape this frozen Hell?' He pictured the soldier under the ice, then saw him again, *in* the ice. Scattered thoughts coalesced in his mind. Eideothea was nibbling at his neck. He grabbed her shoulders. Her face hovered over his, although he could not see it. "Is that the horrible fate you can save me from? To rule—unwisely?"

She did not answer. In the silence his thoughts went to her nude body. To the sensation of her on him. He felt the softness of her skin. It was contrasted by the roughness of her scabs. He realized he had completely forgotten about, and could not even feel, the activity of the flies. He wondered if they were still present. This thought was overrun by a growing sensation.

He could feel her heart beating close to his. It seemed as if their two hearts beat in one body. He knew the location of her mouth. He lifted his head and parted her lips with his own. She twisted her head, forming a loose seal with their lips, and lowered her agile tongue into his mouth. His tongue rose to greet hers.

"You can return to your life," she whispered. She kissed him, passionately, then lifted her head. "You can be prince once more. The people will rejoice at your return."

He returned her kiss. She pulled away. "You can be king. You *will* be king. He can guide you."

"Baalzebul?"

"The Lord of Flies," breathed Eideothea. "The White Son."

"A devil," countered Lewin. He pushed against her, holding her shoulders off of him. "A dark elf witch," he accused her, but his voice held no resolve in it.

"Lewin," whispered Eideothea. "*You* are the White Son. You are the Prince of—" She reached down, sliding her fingers down his abdomen. "Lewin," she whispered. She pressed her body against his. "*My* prince," she breathed. "*My* king."

Lewin pulled her to him. He took her lips in his. She kissed him then lifted her head. She locked eyes with him.

"Take me my king. Conquer me."

. . .

Lewin lay on his side, drifting at the edge of sleep. He held Eideothea's smaller frame in his arms. "Why do you hurt yourself?"

"To honor him," she said, her voice reverent.

"He requires it?"

"What is pleasure without pain?" she asked. "What is loyalty without sacrifice?" She turned her head and brought her hand to his cheek. "Even a king must pay a price. The greatest price of all."

"To suffer for his people?"

"If you wish to lead them, yes. To lead a people is to suffer for them."

The souls trapped in ice came to his mind. "To send men to their deaths."

"To have the resolve to do so, to demand that sacrifice. Only Baalzebul can teach you such strength." She lowered her hand and turned, snuggling closer to him.

"Baalzebul," whispered prince Lewin.

"A great general, a wise leader."

"A fallen angel?"

"A righteous rebel."

"He knew what must be done?"

"He knew," said Eideothea. "He had the courage of his convictions."

"I can't imagine doing as my father did, sending an army against such a treacherous foe."

Eideothea turned her head and looked at him out of the corners of her eyes. "All foes are treacherous." She turned further and kissed him, before turning back.

"I was taught war," said Lewin, speaking almost to himself as much as to her. "I read treaties on battle, spoke to experienced soldiers. I learned about the machinations of court intrigue." Eideothea spun to face him. They looked into each other's eyes. Lewin continued. "I've been schooled on every aspect of rule," he chuckled. "But somehow, I wasn't ready. I—"

"It's all abstract," said Eideothea, reaching up to caress his face, "the reality is—"

"Men died because I failed to—"

"Not you."

"Yes, me. I was in charge," said prince Lewin. "I'm the—"

"General Ord wouldn't have listened to you, even if you had commanded him to do differently than he did. We knew that." She smiled. "Don't forget, we had spies. We knew his character intimately."

"Did you know mine?"

"I do now," said Eideothea.

"No, that's not what I mean," said Lewin. "Did you —plan," he studied her face. "All this?"

"Did I plan on risking my life to snatch you away from bickering demons?" She laughed. "No, my king, that was stupidly impulsive of me." She kissed him then pulled back and looked into his eyes. "No, when I saw you drug in and tossed at their feet, when I looked upon this face," she touched his lips with her fingertips, "I saw the great soul within. It shone even through closed eyes." Lewin had never been spoken to in such a way. He felt a mixture of embarrassment and pride swell up in him. Eideothea was studying him. "I knew you would achieve greatness, if only you received the right—insights."

"Baalzebul?"

"Yes, only he—"

"Can teach me the final lesson," finished Prince Lewin. "The wisdom all my wise instructors couldn't impart?" Eideothea didn't speak, she gazed into his eyes. "But—a devil. How can I—"

"Condemned, yes," said Eideothea. "But by whom? By a just creator? Ask yourself, if there was no injustice, why would there be those willing to risk eternal damnation to rise up?" Lewin had no answer. "I cannot force you to accept my master," said Eideothea. "I can only beg you, for your own sake, to listen to him, to accept his teachings."

Lewin nodded, saying yes with his eyes.

"You—"

"I am prepared to—to accept his wisdom."

Eideothea kissed him. She rolled over and pulled his arms around her. "Your youthful vigor wore me out." She curled into him. Lewin held her in his arms. He rested his head against the furs and closed his eyes. His breathing followed hers. The beating of his heart matched the rhythm of hers.

. . .

"Prince Lewin." The voice was distant, as if whispered from across the room. He stirred but did not open his eyes. "Prince Lewin. Wake up."

Lewin opened his eyes. He realized at once that he was in the cell. The hard, cold, stone floor had replaced the comfort of the furs. There remained, however, a lingering warmth in his arms. 'Eideothea.' He remembered holding her as they fell asleep. He remembered making love to her. He felt for her. Only the stone greeted his hands.

"Eideothea?"

No light came from the slot in the door. He crawled on his hands and knees, searching. His palms found something rich in texture, warm and wet. He could not see the blood on his hands, but he knew it from the smell and touch of it. The blood formed a trail that led to the door.

"Eideothea?" He wiped the blood on his pants and felt around the cell. It was empty. When he reached the door he realized it was not shut tightly, as it had been. The trail of blood led under the door. He edged his fingers into the gap and pulled the door open. The hall was as dark as the cell. He crawled through the door way. His palms and knees slipped in the fresh blood.

"Eideothea?" he called, a bit louder. He heard the striking of a match. A flame leapt from the darkness. He blinked his eyes. The flame went to a candle. He could not tell who had lit the candle. He did, however, hear the person's footsteps as they moved away from him. It was not the sound of hard soles on stone, but of bare feet.

"Eideothea?" His voice echoed back to him. He rose and approached the candle. His bare feet picked up the blood, despite his efforts to avoid it. The candle was in a brass holder, sitting on the floor. He could see the splatter of blood around it. He tried to look down the hall, but saw nothing. He bent and picked up the candle holder. His blood-smeared hand came into view.

'Is this real?' he asked himself. He could feel the feeble heat from the flame, the cold of the stone beneath his feet. He felt the pain of hunger. He felt the ache of fatigue in his muscles and bones. He had never felt such pain and discomfort in a dream. 'More magic?' he asked himself. 'More lies?'

He caught the fragrance of Eideothea on him. The smell of her sex emanated from his body, from his groin, from his fingers, from his lips. These carnal odors mixed with the smell of blood. The mixture clouded his thinking. He shook his head, trying to free his mind from the fog.

He advanced down the hall. It was straight, carved, not natural. The trail of splattered blood continued. The light from his candle crept onto a wooden door. He stared at it in shock. 'I know this door,' he thought. 'My father's crest.' He held the candle closer. He reached out and touched the embossed surface. When he pulled his fingers back the royal crest was streaked with blood.

He looked at the door pull. He reached to it, lifted it, releasing the latch, and pushed the door away from him. Light greeted him. Not sunlight, for the windows in the room were hidden behind thick curtains. The room was illuminated with the light from candles and from the fire in the hearth. He stepped into the room. 'My father's bedroom,' he thought. 'No, not quite.' He realized that there were subtle differences. Things had been moved, a tapestry, a table, an added sitting chair, making two where before there had been one. Other things had been added. A wardrobe, doors open, a woman's dresses spilling out.

He set the candle down on a table. He walked to a window and pulled the curtain back. There was no window pane. In its place was a wall of ice. The life-draining cold reached out to him. He closed the curtain.

"Lewin."

He spun. He saw her for a moment as she stood behind the room's second door. She moved, disappearing from view. "Eideothea!" He ran to the door, flung it fully open, and looked for her. She was gone. What he saw instead was the throne room. 'My father's throne room.'

He passed the threshold and stood, looking. Once again, like the bedroom behind him, there were subtle changes. As if a new occupant had brought their own personal taste to bear. "Eideothea?" He walked into the room. He felt the warmth and slickness of blood. He looked down and saw that the trail continued. His eyes searched the room. "Don't hide from me." He commanded. "You've no need for magic after what we've shared. Dispel this illusion."

He followed the blood, convinced that it was hers. It went to the throne. He stopped and looked down. Sitting on the cushion was a single fly. Its wing lying flat. A leg lifted high, bent, and scrapped the surface of the wing, cleaning it. He reached down, intent on swiping at the fly. An ebony hand grabbed his wrist. He looked.

She smiled at him. He noticed that her skin was unblemished. Her hair was carefully combed and done in plaits. She wore a form-fitting dress, cut low in the front, revealing the curves of her breasts. No flies crawled on her skin. He turned to face her. He looked into her blood-washed eyes.

"This isn't—"

She lifted a finger to his lips. "Shhh," she smiled. "Sit, my king." She looked to the throne. The fly took flight, buzzing between them. Eideothea rested her hands on Lewin's shoulders. She pushed him gently to the throne. Then she climbed into his lap. She leaned into him and began to kiss and bite at the soft skin of his neck. Lewin felt himself weaken at her touch. He wrapped one hand around her, resting the other on the arms of the throne.

Something tickled the ring finger of his free hand. He lifted his hand into view, resting it on the curve of Eideothea's hip. The fly had landed on his finger. It sat there, facing him. 'Where the royal signet ring—' Lewin did not finish his thought. He had the desire to wave his hand, to shake the fly free, but, just as the thought entered his mind, a flash of pain came from his abdomen, where either the guard or Eideothea had jabbed him. He didn't know which was real. The sensation traveled through his body, shuddering him. Just as the pain died down Eideothea took the lobe of his ear between her lips. She began to suck on it. The pleasure, such a contrast to the pain, made Lewin's head swim.

He stared into the fly's compound eyes. His attention turned inwards, to the sensations his body felt, the pleasure from Eideothea's gentle kisses and playful biting. She ran her long, delicate fingers through his hair. Her other hand cupped his neck, pulling him closer to her. "My king," she whispered. "The King of Flies."

Lewin's attention went back to the fly. It was motionless, regarding him with an intensity far beyond the powers of a mere insect. His own multifaceted reflection sunk him into a trance. He blinked. He was staring into Eideothea's fly-eyed mask.

He blinked again and looked at her in totality. She was sitting cross-legged in front of him. He too was sitting cross-legged. The throne room was no more. They sat in the cave in which they had made love. Above them, far above them, above the mountain peak, floated the Lofty House.

Eideothea held her arms out. They were covered with fresh blood and flies. Eideothea was holding something in her hands. Lewin realized she was holding his hands in hers. His arms, too, were extended. His arms, too, were covered in fresh blood and flies. She was chanting, as before, only, unlike before, now he could understand her.

"—took Moloch and Nybbas into his confidence and showed them the way to victory." She was saying. Lewin looked down. He was bare-chested. His torso was covered in blood. "When it came time for the Exodus from Heaven," continued Eideothea, "to break the chains of light, the oppression of the Creator, who lifted the fiery sword? Who struck the first blow? Baalzebul! The White Son!"

The stone of the cave walls flew apart without sound. For a second, blinding white light filled his eyes. It was the light of the ice-coated plain. When his vision returned the light was gone. In its place rose the steep, ice-carved walls of the Lofty House. Eideothea hovered in the foreground, a shimmering, indistinct presence. A second presence came into focus.

He was a perfectly formed being—an angel. He sat, bare chested, his skin as white and pristine as newly fallen snow. His waist was wrapped in white cloth trimmed in gold. He sat on a throne made of ice. His white-blonde hair cascaded over the flawless musculature of his shoulders. He studied Lewin with ice-blue eyes—a blue extended to an infinite depth.

'Baalzebul,' thought Lewin. The presence radiated such inhuman beauty that he was difficult to accept as real. Yet, his eyes, 'his eyes,' thought Lewin. 'So cruel. Completely without compassion.' Just like ice.

Baalzebul leaned forward. His wings unfolded behind him. They were not wings of white feathers. They were without distinct form, merely the suggestion of form, dark, shifting, buzzing. Lewin realized that Baalzebul's wings were composed of thousands, 'No,' he thought, 'hundreds of thousands,' of flies.

The twin clouds of flies changed their shape. They no longer loosely resembled two wings, but became tendrils. With an almost imperceptible nod of Baalzebul's head the tendrils of flies curled. Their tips turned towards Lewin. With a horrifying cacophony of buzzing the tendrils shot out. The flies reached for Lewin. He cringed. They moved past him. He turned to follow their movement. The tips of the fly-composed tendrils moved over a body suspended behind Lewin. The merciless biting of the flies caused the man to scream.

He seemed half alive. He was nude. His head hung so that his dirty, blood-clotted hair—the same color as Lewin's—hid his face. His skin was a tapestry of pain; cuts, bruises, lacerations, welts, flaps of skin hung from his torso. Flies burrowed into his tissue, biting as deep as bone.

"What of those who defy the White Son?" asked Eideothea. "What of those who reject the loving hand of the master?" Her voice was intimate, in contrast to the angry buzzing of the flies and pained screaming of the tortured man. "Do they not hang—bloody, torn, defeated, filled with regret for their treachery—in the Lofty House? Let the foes of Baalzebul think of the tortures that await them should they act against the Lord of Flies. Let those who prove their loyalty to the White Son feed on the betrayer's blood. Let them get fat on his sorrow."

Lewin looked from the half-dead man to the Lord of Flies. A malice-filled smile spread across his perfectly sculpted face. His ice-blue eyes flashed with a sinister light.

"You have accepted him," said Eideothea. "He has accepted you." She squeezed his hands. "You will be king. I will be your queen. I am with child, my King." Lewin's

216

gaze shot from the fallen angel to the dark elf woman gripping his hands. She smiled. The act did not fill him with comfort. "I carry our son." Lewin was so stunned he could not speak. Eideothea continued. "You will rule a nation. You will command a people." Her gaze shifted to Baalzebul. "But he will be master."

A pained cry turned Lewin's attention to the shackled, tortured presence. The man screamed and threw his head back. Lewin looked into the agony-twisted face.

It was his own.

H. Rad Bethlen has been compared to Isak Dinesen (*Seven Gothic Tales*) and Fritz Leiber (*Swords and Deviltry*). He is known for his work in the fantasy and horror genres as well as his non-fiction. He has been published in Europe and America.

Enjoy these stories?

If you liked what you read, please take a moment to **leave a review on Amazon**! Your feedback helps other readers find these stories. It only takes a minute but it makes a huge difference. The Amazon algorithm requires 30-50 reviews before it will pick this book up and promote it to like-minded readers. Your review is instrumental in helping that happen!

For more great fiction and non-fiction please visit:

roosterandravenpublishing.com

hradbethlen.com

or H. Rad Bethlen's Amazon page.

www.ingramcontent.com/pod-product-compliance
Lightning Source LLC
Chambersburg PA
CBHW060434180626
46817CB00007B/2802

* 9 7 8 1 9 6 5 6 5 0 1 6 5 *